Knights Club

The Buried City

SHUKY · WALTCH · NOVY

QUIRK BOOKS
PHILADELPHIA

With exceptional assistance on the story from Netanel, a colossal giant of expertise

Originally published in France as
Chevaliers: La cité ensevelie in 2014 by Makaka Éditions.

First published in the United States in 2020
by Quirk Productions, Inc.

Library of Congress Cataloging in Publication Number:
2019930328

ISBN: 978-1-68369-147-1

Printed in China
Translated by Carol Klio Burrell
Cover design by Elissa Flanigan
Typeset in Sketchnote
Production management by John J. McGurk

Quirk Books
215 Church Street
Philadelphia, PA 19106
quirkbooks.com

10 9 8 7 6 5 4 3 2 1

Halt!

THIS ISN'T A REGULAR COMIC BOOK!

In this comic book, you don't read straight through from first page to the last. Instead, you'll begin at the beginning and soon be off on a quest where *you* choose which panel to read next. You'll go on an adventure, answer riddles, solve puzzles, and face down mighty foes—because YOU are the main character!

It's easy to get the hang of it once you see it in action. Turn the page to see an example of how this comic book plays like a game!

HOW TO PLAY COMIC QUESTS

1 First pick where you want to go—doors, paths, signs, and objects can all have numbers, so keep your eyes peeled!

2 Flip to the panel with the matching number.

3 Continue reading from there, making more choices as you go to complete the quest!

HOW TO PLAY COMIC QUESTS

As you go, use the handy Quest Tracker sheets on the next few pages to log your progress. Use a pencil so you can erase. (You can also use a notebook and pencil, or download extra sheets at comicquests.com.)

THE RULES OF KNIGHTHOOD

While playing the game, be sure to follow these rules to preserve your honor as a knight.

REMAIN VIGILANT: Always examine your surroundings for hidden passages, objects, and people—they may be hard to spot.

KNOW YOUR ATTACK: Your weapon or your spell will have a certain number of attack points that you can keep track of on your Quest Tracker. If you get new weapons or spells, their points will wipe out and replace the ones you have, so choose wisely.

STAY TRUE TO YOUR STRENGTHS: You may carry only as many objects as you have strength points. However, you can unload an object whenever you need to make room for a new one. Your main weapon, jewelry, armor, and clothes don't count against your strength points. Your purse can hold up to 98 gold pieces—but no more!

KEEP TRACK OF YOUR PROGRESS: Your Quest Tracker has squares to represent your Experience points (XP) and your Strike points (SP). When you have enough XP to level up, you'll gain the corresponding amount of SP for that level, and a special ability point you can use for strength, agility, or intelligence. Only a potion or leveling up will get you back your lost SP!

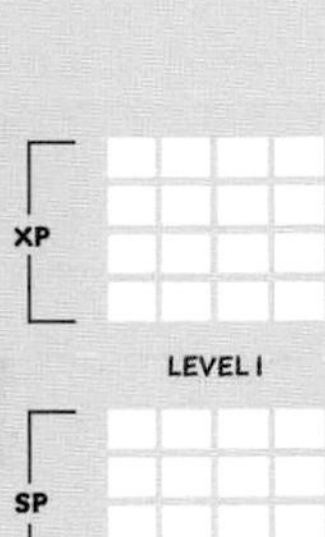

FIGHT WITH HONOR: Use the combat wheel at the end of the book to fight enemies when they appear. The effectiveness of your attacks and spells will be determined by how you turn the wheel. Fight through the first battle in the beginning of the book to learn how combat works!

GOOD LUCK! LET THE ADVENTURE BEGIN . . .

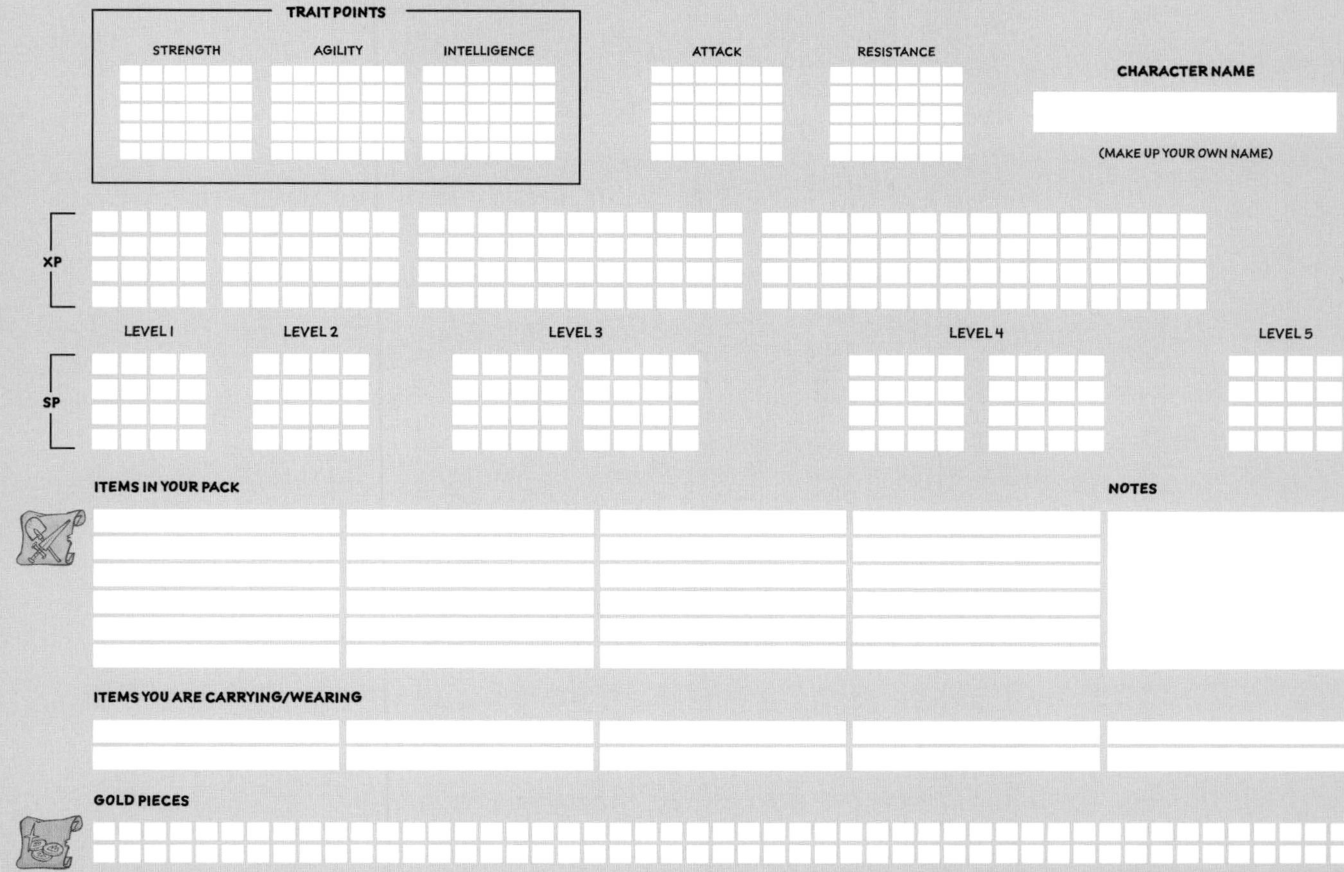
Quest Tracker
TRAIT POINTS
STRENGTH
AGILITY
INTELLIGENCE
ATTACK
RESISTANCE
CHARACTER NAME
(MAKE UP YOUR OWN NAME)
XP
LEVEL 1
LEVEL 2
LEVEL 3
LEVEL 4
LEVEL 5
SP
ITEMS IN YOUR PACK
NOTES
ITEMS YOU ARE CARRYING/WEARING
GOLD PIECES

Quest Tracker

TRAIT POINTS

STRENGTH

AGILITY

INTELLIGENCE

ATTACK

RESISTANCE

CHARACTER NAME

(MAKE UP YOUR OWN NAME)

XP

LEVEL 1

LEVEL 2

LEVEL 3

LEVEL 4

LEVEL 5

SP

ITEMS IN YOUR PACK

NOTES

ITEMS YOU ARE CARRYING/WEARING

GOLD PIECES

Quest Tracker

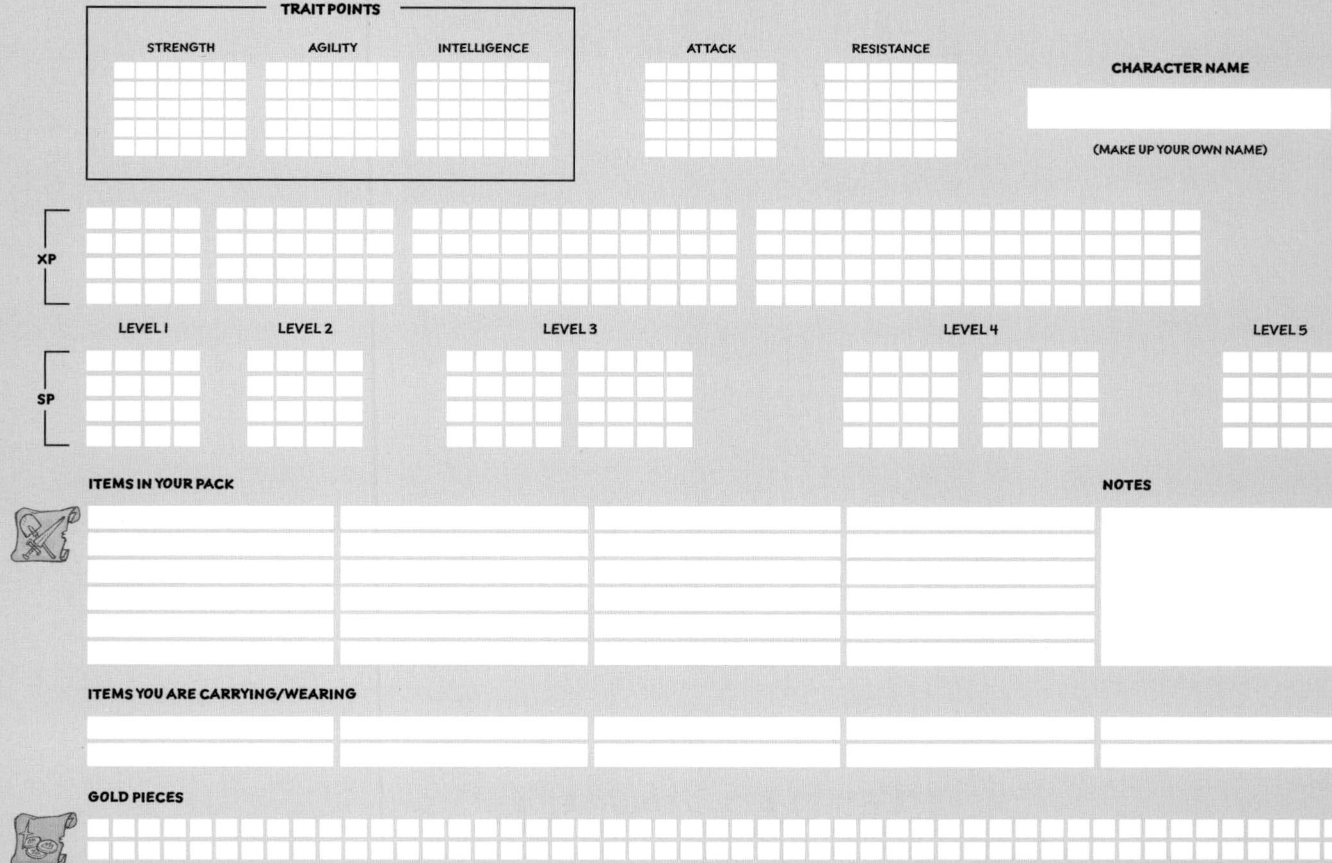

Quest Tracker

TRAIT POINTS

STRENGTH

AGILITY

INTELLIGENCE

ATTACK

RESISTANCE

CHARACTER NAME

(MAKE UP YOUR OWN NAME)

XP

LEVEL 1

LEVEL 2

LEVEL 3

LEVEL 4

LEVEL 5

SP

ITEMS IN YOUR PACK

NOTES

ITEMS YOU ARE CARRYING/WEARING

GOLD PIECES

List of Hidden Treasures

These are the items you need to collect on your adventure.

Emerald-encrusted tiara

Eagle-headed scepter

Glass bow

Black-iron sword

Pink-pearl necklace

Gold-thread bracelet

Statuette

Dog helmet

Vase

Ruby

The tricky fish

The golden platter

Begin Your Quest!

And now your adventure begins, bold knight! Choose your character, cut out your Quest Tracker or download one from comicquests.com, and go on to the next page.

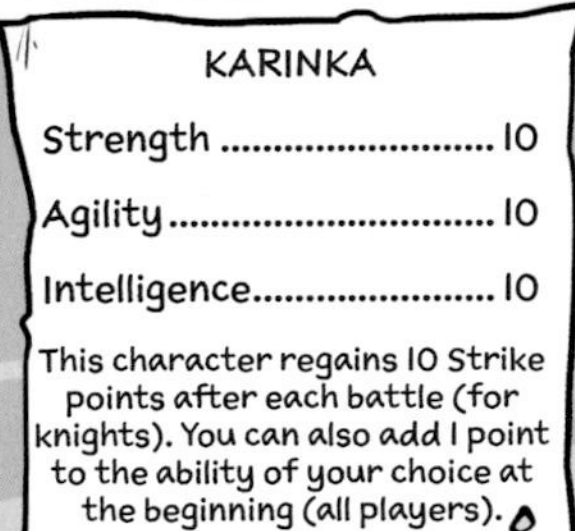

KARINKA

Strength 10

Agility 10

Intelligence 10

This character regains 10 Strike points after each battle (for knights). You can also add 1 point to the ability of your choice at the beginning (all players).

FIGHTER

Strength 14

Agility 8

Intelligence 8

This character adds 1 point to Attack or Resistance at each new level (for knights). For squires, this character adds 2 more Attack points after every 5 foes battled.

Equipped item: Sword (+3 Attack points)

Equipped item: Shield (+1 Resistance points)

MAGE (cannot use weapons)

Strength 5

Agility 8

Intelligence 17

This character has the ability to recognize certain plants for making potions. If you choose, go to 52 in order to learn how to recognize these plants (knights only). The Mage can also tame some creatures (all players).

ARCHER

Strength 10

Agility 10

Intelligence 10

This character can strike twice at the beginning of a battle, spinning the wheel twice (knights only). The Archer can also pick certain locks (all players).

You'll find the list of items to collect on the page following your Quest Tracker.
Next move on to page 15.

This sure is a strange way to start an adventure . . . and now you have your first choice to make. Do you want to swim to shore and avoid Harold (panel 13), or would you rather ask him to help you get to the dock (panel 143)?

1
47
125
25
If you're coming from pañel 47, and you've never been here and want to go to the trading town, go to 69.

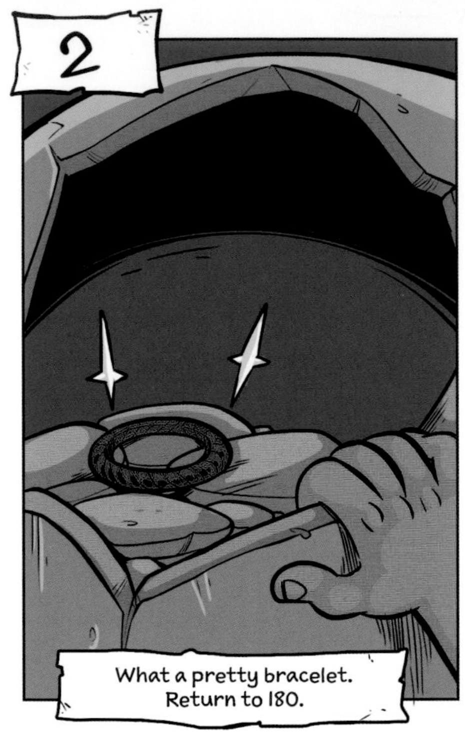
2
What a pretty bracelet. Return to 180.

3
I told you! The answer was so easy because there's absolutely nothing to see in this room. Return to 207.

4
162
189

5
If you have the key with the eagle's head, go to 82. If not, you can come back here whenever you have the key in your possession. Return to 209.

6
A dead end! Go back to 218, unless you have more than 12 Strength points. In that case, you can slam into the wall with your shoulder and break through to the other side in 184.

7
You can take this corridor to panel 182 or go back to 15.

8
=5
112
207

9
157

10
104

11
199

12
161

13

That swim was exhausting! You lose 5 Strike points. What's worse, you're starting off your adventure in the middle of the jungle. You could still go into town, but you risk getting caught by Harold.

91→

136

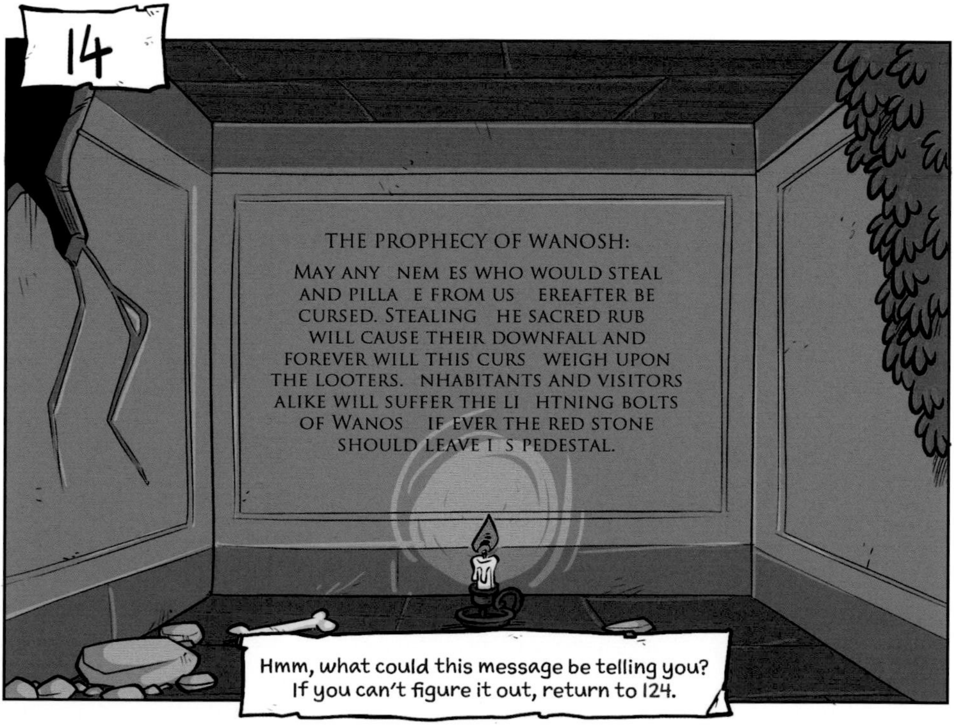

14

THE PROPHECY OF WANOSH:

MAY ANY NEM ES WHO WOULD STEAL
AND PILLA E FROM US EREAFTER BE
CURSED. STEALING HE SACRED RUB
WILL CAUSE THEIR DOWNFALL AND
FOREVER WILL THIS CURS WEIGH UPON
THE LOOTERS. NHABITANTS AND VISITORS
ALIKE WILL SUFFER THE LI HTNING BOLTS
OF WANOS IF EVER THE RED STONE
SHOULD LEAVE I S PEDESTAL.

Hmm, what could this message be telling you? If you can't figure it out, return to 124.

15

124

174

7

16

What a mess. But maybe you can "read" your way to a clue? If not, return to 207.

17

172

129

18

This door is solidly shut. If you have more than 15 Intelligence points, go to 196. If you don't, you won't be able to solve the puzzle on this door, so return to 104.

19

32

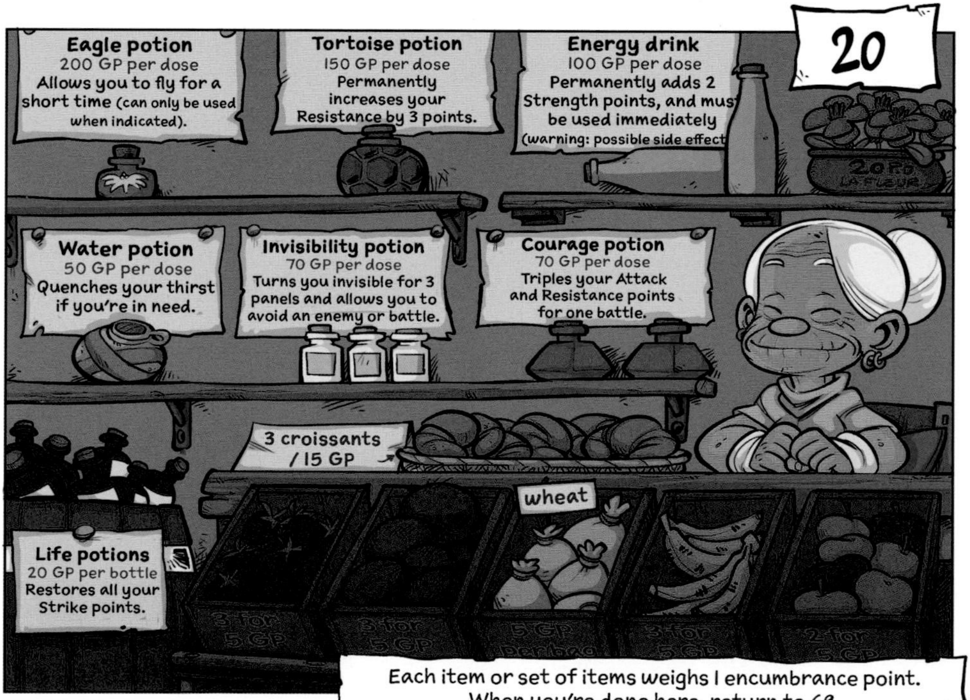

20

Eagle potion
200 GP per dose
Allows you to fly for a short time (can only be used when indicated).

Tortoise potion
150 GP per dose
Permanently increases your Resistance by 3 points.

Energy drink
100 GP per dose
Permanently adds 2 Strength points, and mus
be used immediately
(warning: possible side effect

Water potion
50 GP per dose
Quenches your thirst if you're in need.

Invisibility potion
70 GP per dose
Turns you invisible for 3 panels and allows you to avoid an enemy or battle.

Courage potion
70 GP per dose
Triples your Attack and Resistance points for one battle.

3 croissants / 15 GP

wheat

Life potions
20 GP per bottle
Restores all your Strike points.

3 for 5 GP

3 for 5 GP

5 GP per bag

3 for 5 GP

2 for 5 GP

Each item or set of items weighs 1 encumbrance point.
When you're done here, return to 69.

21

176

22

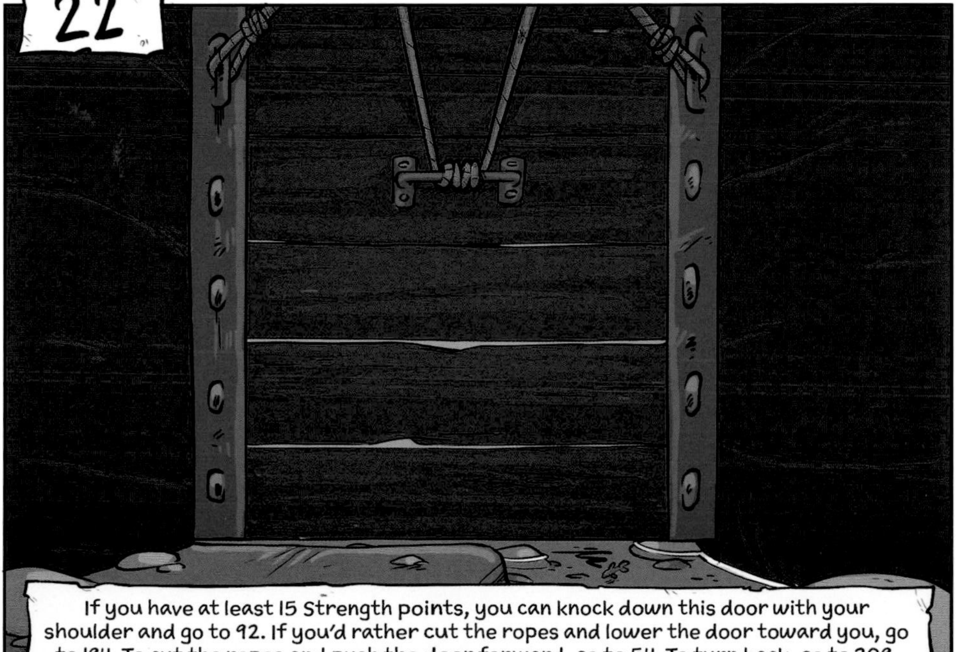

If you have at least 15 Strength points, you can knock down this door with your shoulder and go to 92. If you'd rather cut the ropes and lower the door toward you, go to 194. To cut the ropes and push the door forward, go to 54. To turn back, go to 209.

23

If you have an empty container, you can catch the fish of your choice and keep it (or do something else with it if you have any ideas). Then return to 40.

24

Someone really wanted to keep you from going any farther. To pass, you must count the number of triangles in this drawing, and then multiply that number by 3. If you can't solve it, return to 15.

25

MULT 3
SP 7 SQ 2
ATT 4
RES 0
SR 0
XP 4
LOOT 0
30
34
175

If this is your first battle, here are some instructions:

Cut out the combat wheel in the back of the book or spin a crayon or pencil around the wheel instead. Use the wheel for battles as shown on the same page.

If you're a squire, only the XP box matters. Your Attack points must be equal to or higher than that number. If they aren't—run away!

You can choose to run away in any case (as you can for most battle encounters). You'll find out if fleeing came at a price in the next panel. If nothing is mentioned, you got away without any trouble.

If you win, you get 4 Experience points, which you note on your Quest Tracker. If you're a squire, you win 5 gold pieces (GP).

Take note! If you're using your character from the previous book in the Comic Quest series, you have to multiply everything by the multiplier (MULT), which in this case is 3. That gives this critter 21 Strike points and 12 Attack points, but doesn't give you extra Experience points or gold pieces, unfortunately.

26

Finally . . . You've made it! That wasn't so bad, but it was only the beginning! From here on, be very careful. Traps and enemies lie in wait. Treasures won't just jump into you backpack on their own. Good luck!

137

27
I am prepared to give you the map that will lead you to the hidden city, but first you must unravel this puzzle. I will be waiting for you at the right panel. If you don't find me after two tries, look for me in panel 214.
This symbol will be found at the panel that you should be going to. If it isn't there, you haven't found the right answer.

28
146

29
Apparently you didn't know that a skeleton isn't the sort of person you can chitchat with. With his sharp blade, your foe slices off your head in one blow. You must begin your adventure again . . .

30
198

MULT	4		
SP	7	SQ	3
ATT	5		
RES	0		
SR	0		
XP	8		
LOOT	10 Gold Pieces		

A guard has spotted you. He had time to give a shout that has alerted his buddies. That makes your search counter go up by 1 Star. The more stars you have, the more chance of getting caught. At any time, you can decide to end your adventure and to 145—and if your counter reaches 5 search stars, you MUST go to 145 . . . But maybe it would be best to get out of this city before that happens? Up to you. For now—the battle is on!

33
If you can pick locks or if you have the eagle-head key, go to 73. Otherwise, go to 167.

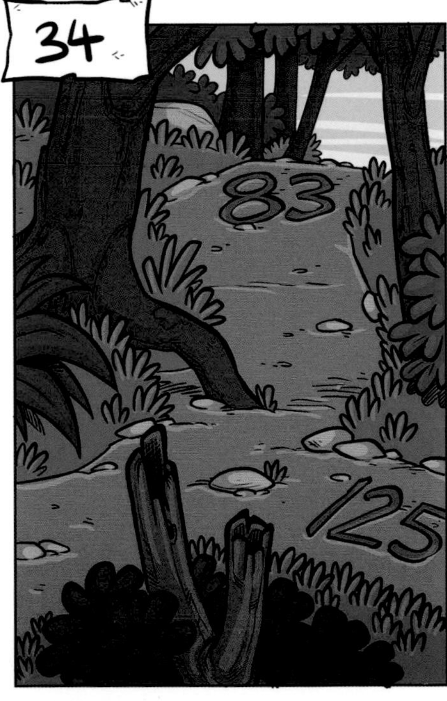

35
This outfit allows you to disguise your appearance and lower your search stars by 1. You can go back to 72.

36
209

37
Looks like your adventure has started off right! Now go to page 1.

38
85

39
MULT 4
SP 7 SQ 3
ATT 5
RES 0
SR 0
XP 8
LOOT 10 Gold Pieces
15
You can choose not to fight and retrace your path to 150, but your search counter will go up by 1 Star. Also, you'll surely have to come back this way some other time. Choose carefully.

40
133

41
You can go back to 197.
Note that you won't be able to open this casket again.

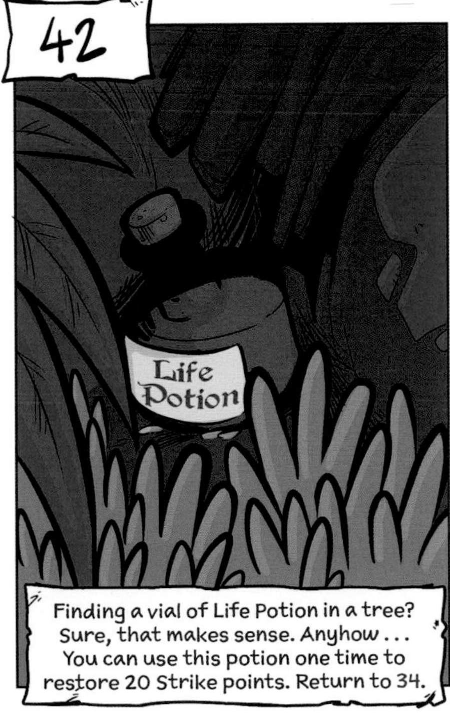
42
Life Potion
Finding a vial of Life Potion in a tree? Sure, that makes sense. Anyhow . . . You can use this potion one time to restore 20 Strike points. Return to 34.

43

If you have over 12 Intelligence points or if you're a squire, go to 56.
If you can't figure out the door puzzle, go back to 207.

44

Squires, you can go to 56 for a hint.
If you still don't get it, return to 150.

45

MULT	4		
SP	11	SQ	3
ATT	8		
RES	1		
SR	0		
XP	8		
LOOT	10 Gold Pieces		

Your foe has seen you before you have a chance to react. He gets the first blow. Subtract it from your Strike points and strike back. Fleeing to 209 is possible, but you'll lose 20 Strike points and 20 Experience points. Squires lose an item (your choice) from your pack. If you run, your search counter goes up by 1 Star.

46

What a strong knight! Slamming into the gate knocked off some bones. Perhaps that helps? Different method, same result.

If you're still blocked, go to 209 or return to the entrance to the city in 150.

47

117

48

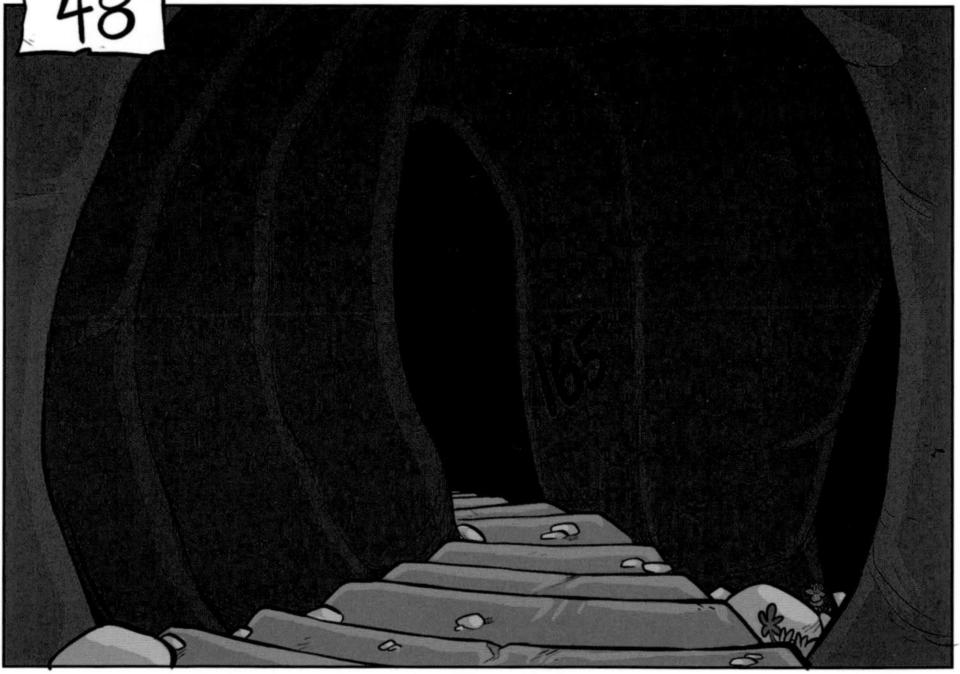

165

49

You can go back to 209.

50

Are you sure you want to take this gem? If you've completely thought it through, go to 108. If you'd rather leave the ruby where it is, go to 187.

51

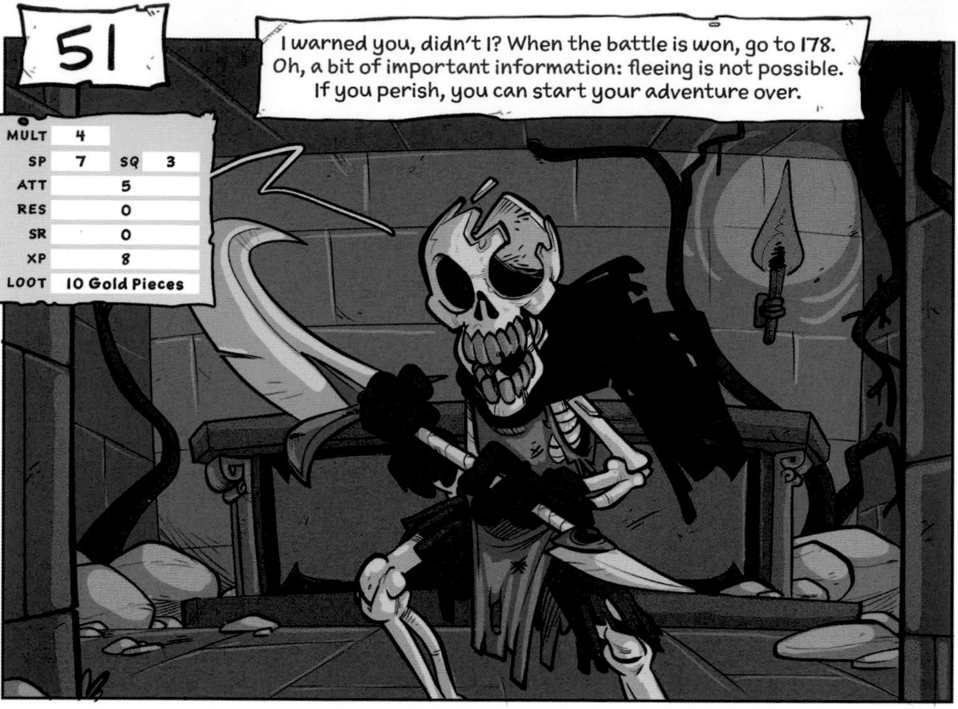

I warned you, didn't I? When the battle is won, go to 178.
Oh, a bit of important information: fleeing is not possible.
If you perish, you can start your adventure over.

MULT	4		
SP	7	SQ	3
ATT	5		
RES	0		
SR	0		
XP	8		
LOOT	10 Gold Pieces		

52

At the dawn of time, our ancestors cured many ills with beneficial herbs and plants that flourished throughout the realm. Some plants, such as wolfsbane, are still common, and most notably replenish one's energy and vigor. Others are more rare, and can be used to prepare mixtures of extraordinary power, if they are combined with the correct other plants.

These plants are extremely light, so you can collect as much of each as you want.

Wolfsbane Caput

smurfuum

Pixius poppius

Urtica stingicus

+ = +1 resistance point

+ + = Complete healing

+ + = +10 Experience points

+ + = +1 to characteristic of your choice

= ?

Once you've memorized these recipes, return to page 3.

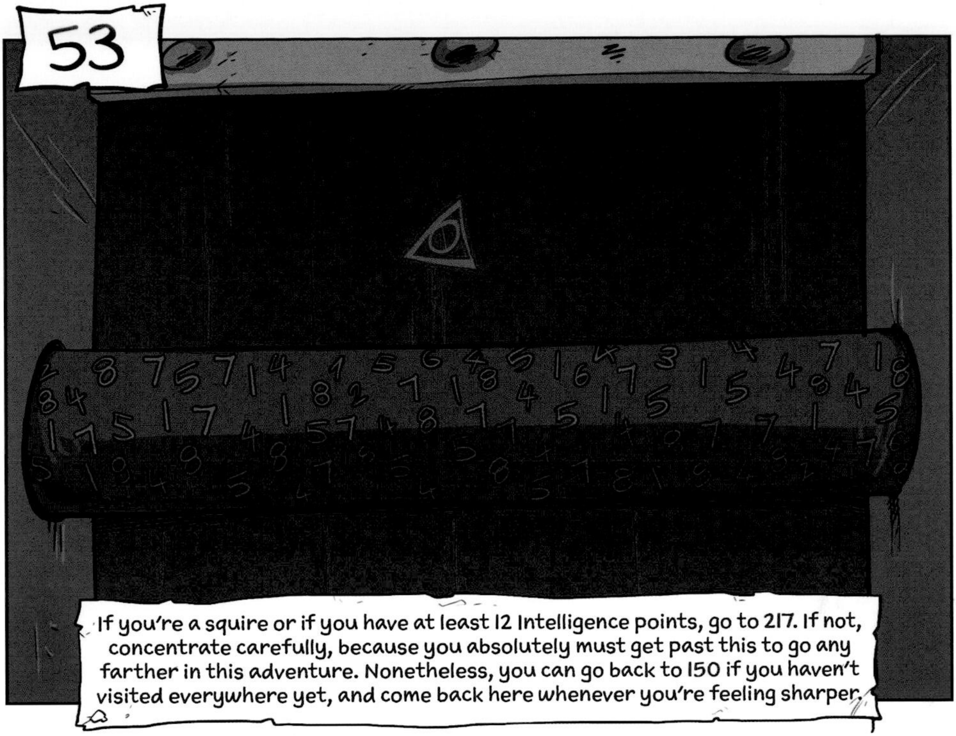

53

If you're a squire or if you have at least 12 Intelligence points, go to 217. If not, concentrate carefully, because you absolutely must get past this to go any farther in this adventure. Nonetheless, you can go back to 150 if you haven't visited everywhere yet, and come back here whenever you're feeling sharper.

54

Well done, good knight! You can cross to 66.

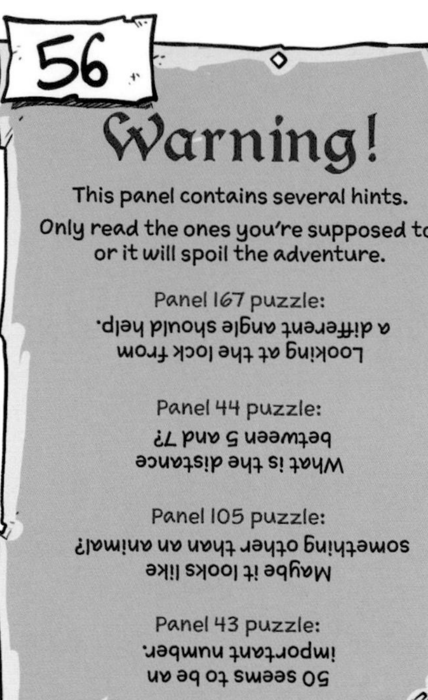

56
Warning!
This panel contains several hints.
Only read the ones you're supposed to, or it will spoil the adventure.
Panel 167 puzzle:
Looking at the lock from a different angle should help.
Panel 44 puzzle:
What is the distance between 5 and 7?
Panel 105 puzzle:
Maybe it looks like something other than an animal?
Panel 43 puzzle:
50 seems to be an important number.

57
Aren't you the knight the guards were after, at the entrance to the city?
All right . . . I can unbolt the gate for you in exchange for a pack of cards or one or two dice. I'm dying of boredom in this place. I need something to amuse myself with.

If you have such an item in your possession and want to give it to him, go to 202. You can also stun him if you have more than 12 Strength points and then go to 62, or you can go back to 15. Warning! You can't secretly steal his keys now because he's watching you. (That's just common sense!)

MULT	4		
SP	9	SQ	2
ATT	5		
RES	0		
SR	0		
XP	8		
LOOT	5 Gold Pieces		

This monkey isn't blocking your way, but he has a character card, so you can fight him if you want. That way you'd avoid a surprise attack in the next panel, but it might be pointless, since it's possible the monkey won't react if you ignore him.

59

This bracelet adds 2 points to each of your abilities. Congrats! Return to 74.

60

Michael . . .
Miiiichael . . .

You can approach the merchant by going to panel 193, or leave the shop in panel 69.

61

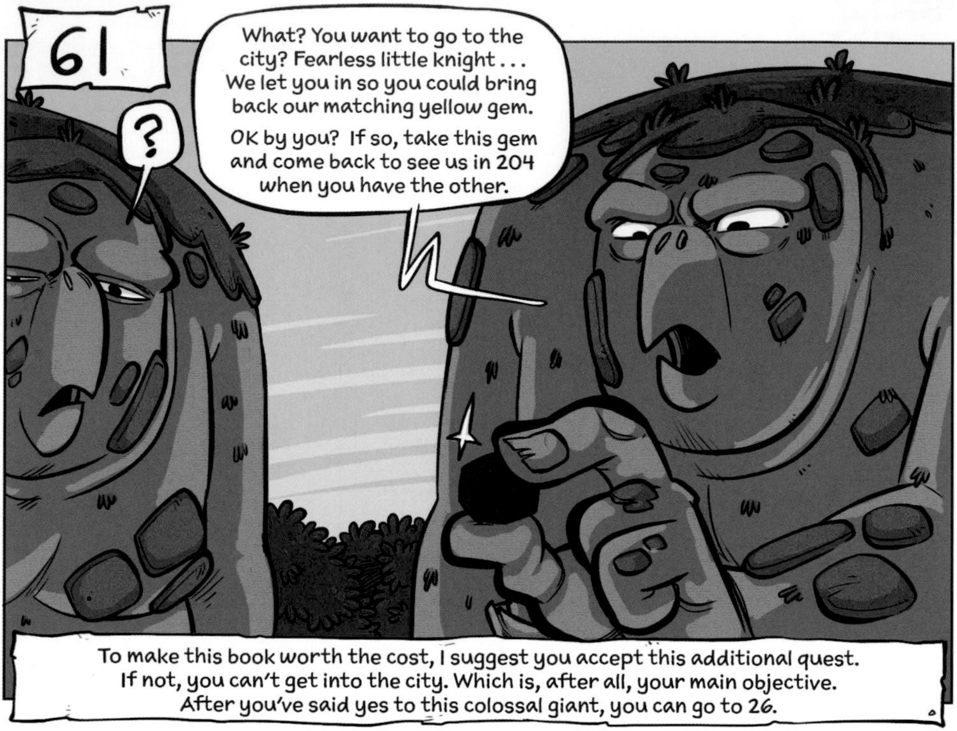

?
What? You want to go to the city? Fearless little knight . . . We let you in so you could bring back our matching yellow gem.
OK by you? If so, take this gem and come back to see us in 204 when you have the other.

To make this book worth the cost, I suggest you accept this additional quest. If not, you can't get into the city. Which is, after all, your main objective. After you've said yes to this colossal giant, you can go to 26.

62

You've unbolted the gate and can go to 149. You can hold onto the key, but it weighs 1 Encumbrance point. If you decide to keep it, go to 140 to find out what kind of lock it opens. Then come back here.

63

MULT	4		
SP	7	SQ	4
ATT	14		
RES	2		
SR	0		
XP	20		
LOOT	30 Gold Pieces		

Whoa! This guy looks ready for a fight! Also, his groaning has raised your search counter by 1 Star. On top of it all, you can't even run away. If you defeat him, go to 102.

64

It's not unlikely that one of the treasures can be found hidden in this room. Search it well, then go back to 150 when you're done.

65

If you chose the [lock icon] character, you can pick the lock and go in to 179. Unless you've found the correct key to open this door?

66

Return to 209.

67

MULT	4		
SP	11	SQ	3
ATT	8		
RES	1		
SR	0		
XP	8		
LOOT	10 Gold Pieces		

Nice throw! The shock has taken 10 Strike points off your adversary and you can now strike an additional blow by spinning the wheel. If you win this battle, go to 135. If you have to flee, go to 209 but lose 5 Strike points and 5 Experience points, and add 1 Star to the search counter.

68

There aren't a million ways past this gate . . . but there are at least four.

You can ask the gentleman on guard to open it and let you through in 57.

If you have more than 12 Agility points and you stealthily swipe the key, you can open the gate and go to 120.

If you have more than 12 Strength points, you can clonk the guard on the head and steal the key in 62.

You can take no risks and go back the other way to 15.

69

Before you head off adventuring in the jungle, I'd advise you to gear up in these little shops. If this is your first adventure in the Knights Club series or if you want to start a new Quest Tracker, your purse contains 50 gold pieces.

Marco's Pl
119

20

70

You need to run fast. Very fast.
You definitely have to drop one of the treasures you're carrying, then bolt to 219.

71

Another foe! This one has an extra feature: 1 Resistance point. You have to subtract 1 point when you make a hit. If you have 5 Attack points, you will only cause 4 points of damage. Note to adventurers using your character from the previous book: Don't forget to multiply by the multiplier (MULT). Your foe will have 3 Resistance points, 24 Strike points, and 12 Attack points. Now go fight!

MULT	3		
SP	8	SQ	2
ATT	4		
RES	1		
SR	0		
XP	3		
LOOT	0		

55

72

186

If you have a grappling hook or an Eagle potion, you can get to the other side of the room in 109. If you just have a rope, you need at least 9 Agility points to try to cross. Warning: it's risky.

73

101

You can eat some fruit, which will restore all your Strike points and give you 10 Experience points. (Organic fruit is good for you!) You can return to 150 if you're finished with this room.

74

127

75

121

208

76

Why oh why didn't you look for a way out? A thirst for gold and adventure drove you to keep exploring the city? Oh well, let this be a lesson . . . Game over!

77
Oh! a letter from Gary, the love of my life! Thank you, good knight. Could you go tell him that I'll meet him in two moons at our usual place?
If you accept, go to 114. You can also go back to 161.

80

MULT	3		
SP	8	SQ	2
ATT	4		
RES	1		
SR	0		
XP	5		
LOOT	0		

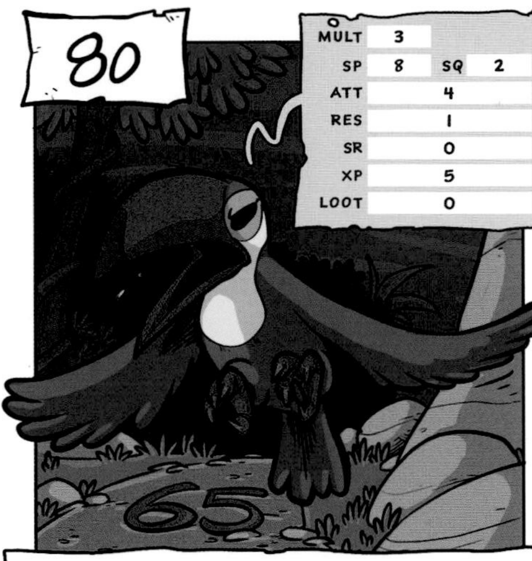

Yikes, another enemy . . . and one with 1 Resistance point. You must subtract 1 point when you make a hit. If you have 5 Attack points, you will only cause 4 points of damage

Adventurers using your character from the previous book, don't forget the multiplier (MULT)—your foe will have 3 Resistance points, 24 Strike points, and 12 Attack points. Now, off you go!

81
33
You can use this bow if you have more than 15 Agility points. It gives you 7 Attack points. The tips of these five arrows are poisoned. They will stun your enemy if you get a hit and allow you to make a second attack. Note: Each arrow can only be used once, but whenever you want.

82
Go back to 209.

83
55
139

84
Looks like you had a lucky escape. You can continue to 159.

85

86

300
No point trying to solve this puzzle: you'll waste the whole day. It is, in fact, a clue. If during your adventure you find this symbol somewhere, deduct 300 from the number you find nearby. Go back to 73.

87

X
X
4
X
9
8
1
2
7
5
4
X
1

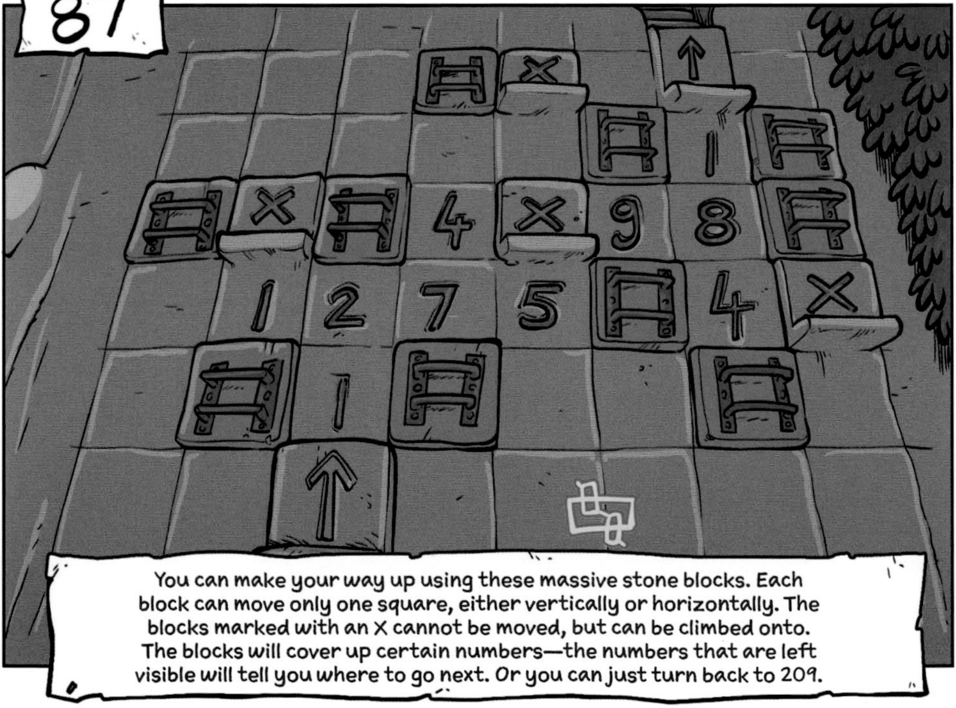

You can make your way up using these massive stone blocks. Each block can move only one square, either vertically or horizontally. The blocks marked with an X cannot be moved, but can be climbed onto. The blocks will cover up certain numbers—the numbers that are left visible will tell you where to go next. Or you can just turn back to 209.

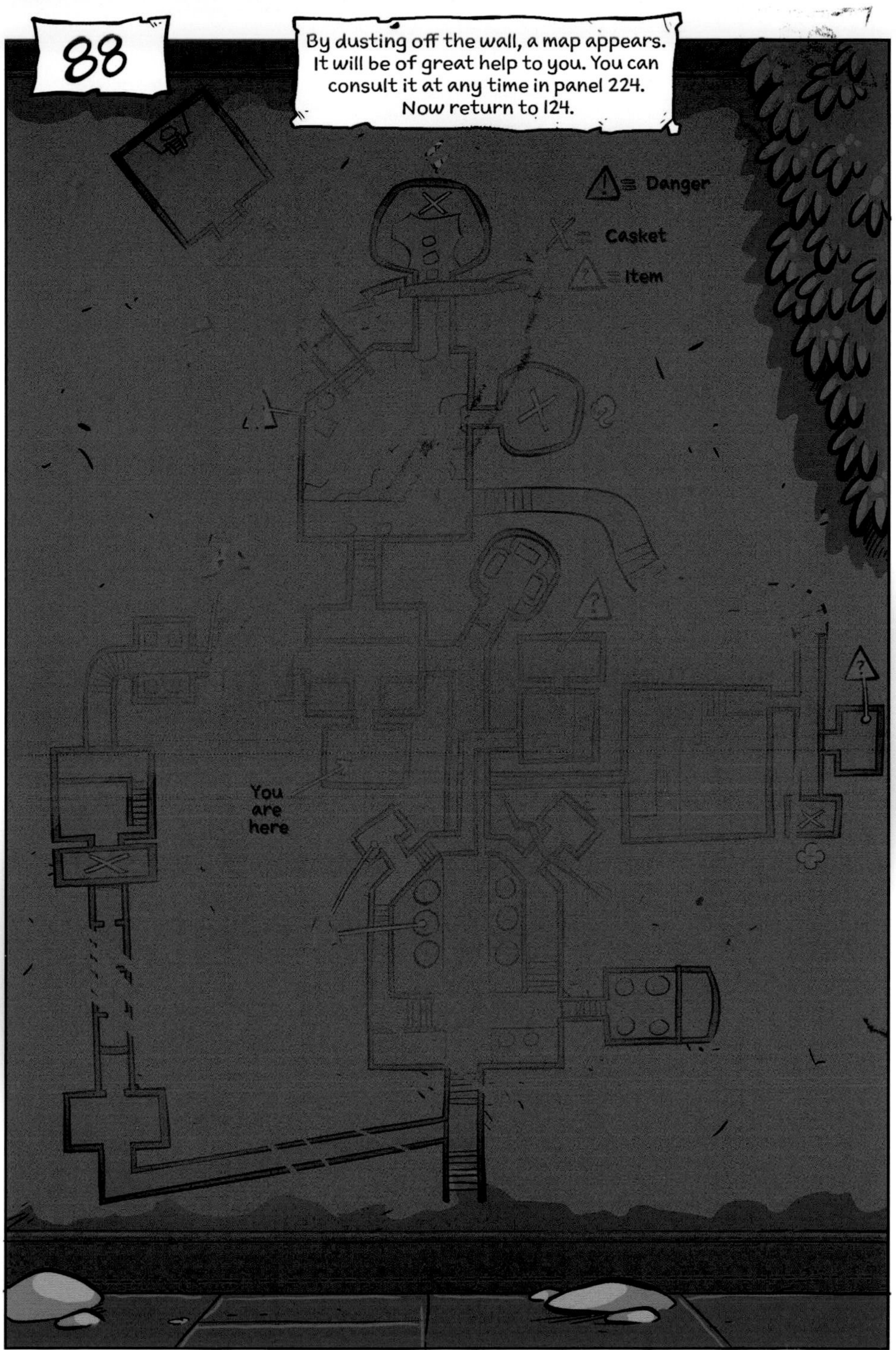
88
By dusting off the wall, a map appears. It will be of great help to you. You can consult it at any time in panel 224. Now return to 124.
Danger
Casket
Item
You are here

89

Think it over, knight! Without me, you'll be wandering around in this jungle for 50 panels . . . but I can show you the way for 50 gold pieces. If you agree, meet me in 113.

If you'd rather trek down the mountain . . . well, stumble down, go to 151. However, you will lose 10 Strike points (10 gold pieces if you're a squire) if you have lower than 14 Agility points.

90

171

11

91
What a dolt you are! You could have drowned carrying all that gear. Follow me to 27. I have something that could be useful on your quest.

92
And to think that you nearly broke your shoulder for that! Go back to 209.

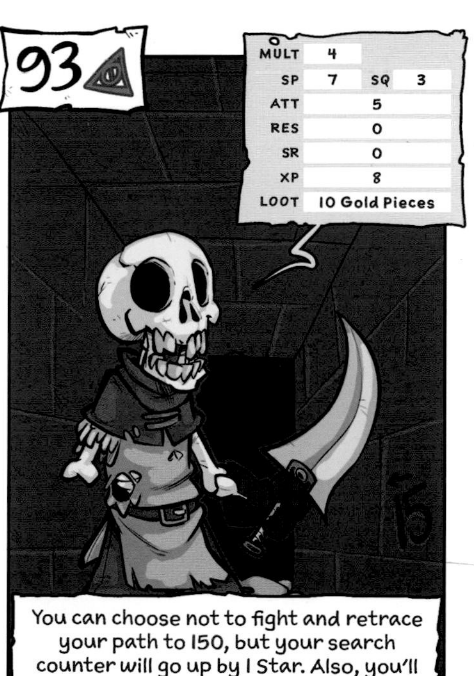
93
MULT 4
SP 7 SQ 3
ATT 5
RES 0
SR 0
XP 8
LOOT 10 Gold Pieces
You can choose not to fight and retrace your path to 150, but your search counter will go up by 1 Star. Also, you'll surely have to come back this way some other time. Choose carefully.

94
195
You can go back down to 150.

95

131
133

96

What are you doing here, vermin? You're looking for the treasure too, is that it?
It's mine! Mine, you hear me?! If you want to pass, you'll have to go through me!
24

MULT	4		
SP	10	SQ	4
ATT	10		
RES	1		
SR	0		
XP	10		
LOOT	20 Gold Pieces		

That leaves no doubt that this is the next place you need to go . . .

If you want to get past, fight. You can flee and retrace your path by returning to 15 (that's a long way back, I know). If you do, you lose 15 gold pieces.

97

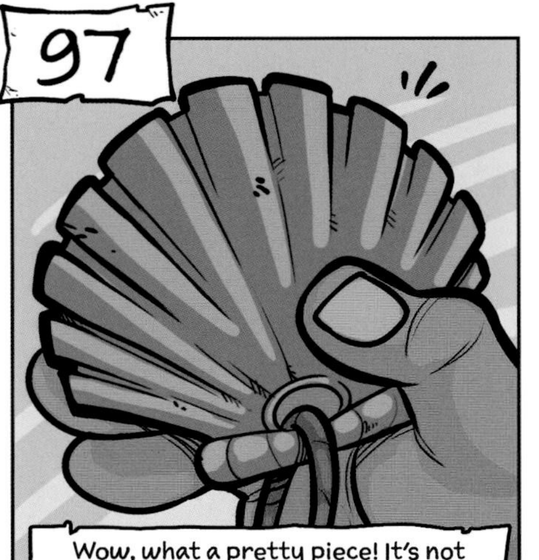

Wow, what a pretty piece! It's not a necklace of invulnerability, but it allows you to increase your Resistance by 3 points. Since this is an item you can wear, it adds no weight. Note! If you're already wearing a necklace, you have to make a choice to leave one behind or put it in your pack, if there's room (in which case, it will weigh 1 Encumbrance point). Now go to 40.

98

He looks so peaceful. Close the tomb back up and go to 15, or head to 150 if you want to return to the entrance to the city.

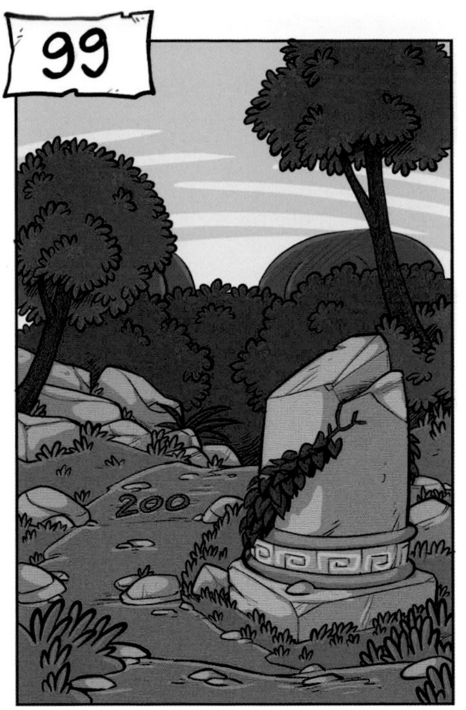

100
Combat Techniques for
Elk Clan Fighters
The threat of a curse won't stop the worst of the looters. Wanosh taught his fighters the most ancient combat techniques to protect the city's legendary treasure. To steal it was dangerous, but merely trying to get close to it was even more so.
You have learned a new combat technique. You win 2 Attack points. Return to 8.

101

You can go back to 73.

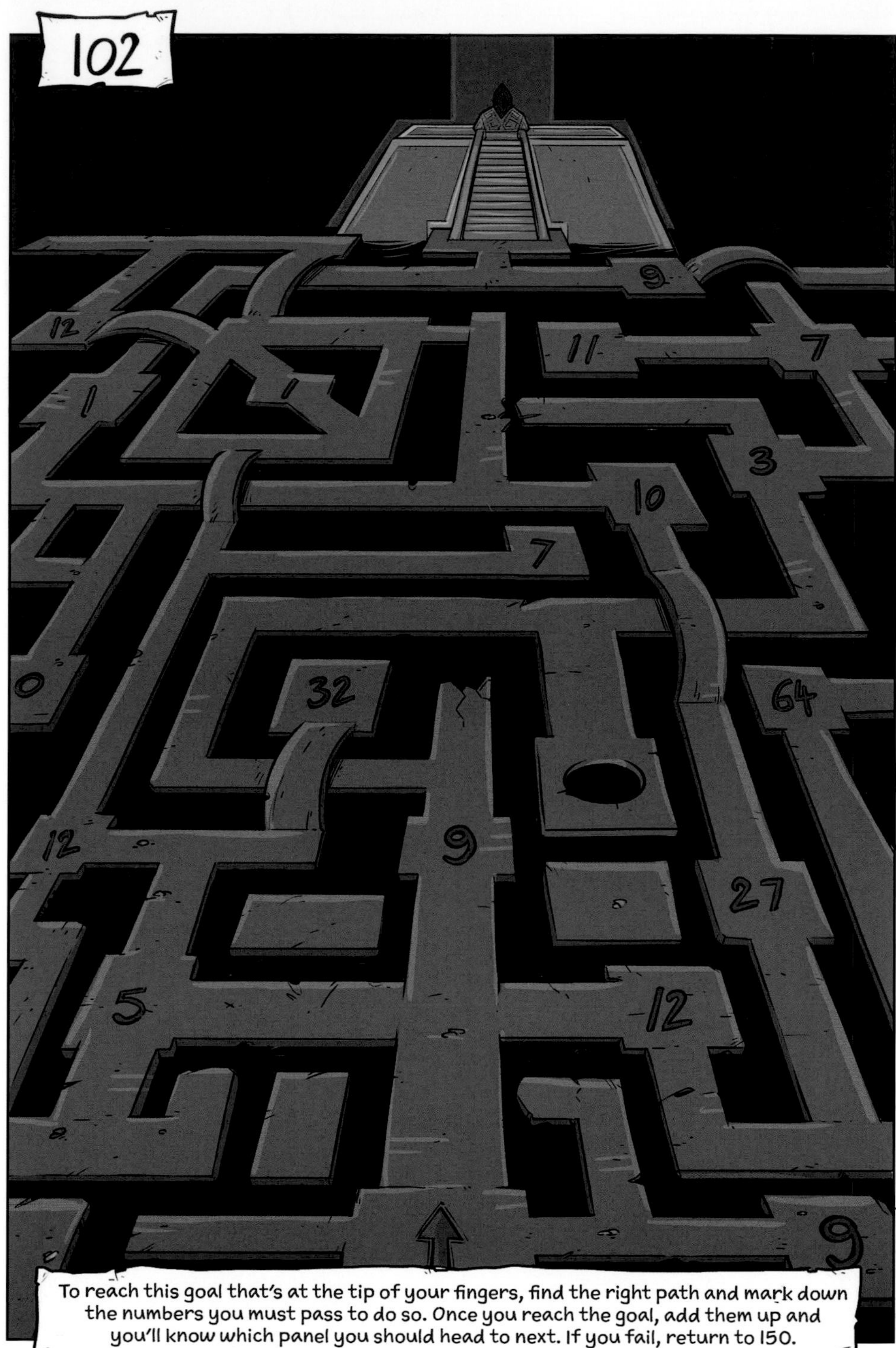
102
9
12
11
7
1
3
10
7
32
64
12
9
27
5
12
9
To reach this goal that's at the tip of your fingers, find the right path and mark down the numbers you must pass to do so. Once you reach the goal, add them up and you'll know which panel you should head to next. If you fail, return to 150.

MULT	4		
SP	7	SQ	3
ATT	5		
RES	0		
SR	0		
XP	8		
LOOT	10 Gold Pieces		

If you have more than 10 items in your pack, you're about as stealthy as a giant in a jungle. The guard turns around, and you must engage in combat. If you win, go to 209. If you have 10 items or fewer, a good knockout blow to the jaw lets you go straight to 36. In any case, there's a lot of noise, and any nearby guards are on alert. Your search counter goes up by 1 Star.

The passageway seems to be blocked! But you'll have to find a way through. If you have at least 10 Agility or if you're a squire, go to 56. You can turn around and go back to 150, but at some point you'll have to come back here.

107

108

Go on to 177.

109

Your little stunt has cost you dearly! If you have lower than 15 Agility points, you lose 10 Strike points—but you gain 1 Agility point. Totally worth it! Getting back to the most interesting part: If you have the wolf-head key or can pick locks, you can open the chest in 35. But if not, you have to go back to 72.

110

Well done, knight! You've earned this. I invite you to gear up in our shops by going to 69.
And don't forget to stop in at Marco's if you want to take back a souvenir of our island. All our goods are tax-free, so it would be a shame not to take advantage!

You can consult the map at 223. Note! You have not yet found the map that's on the other side, in 224. Don't look at it or you'll spoil the adventure.

111
You can take a rest in 154 or continue climbing up in 183. You can also go back to 150 if you're getting dizzy.

112

113
123

114
Knight, you're a person of your word. To thank you, I give you this bow. I won it in a game a little while ago, but I don't know what I'd do with it. Maybe it'll be useful to you.
You can return to the Hall of Alchemists (161) or the Main Hall (150).

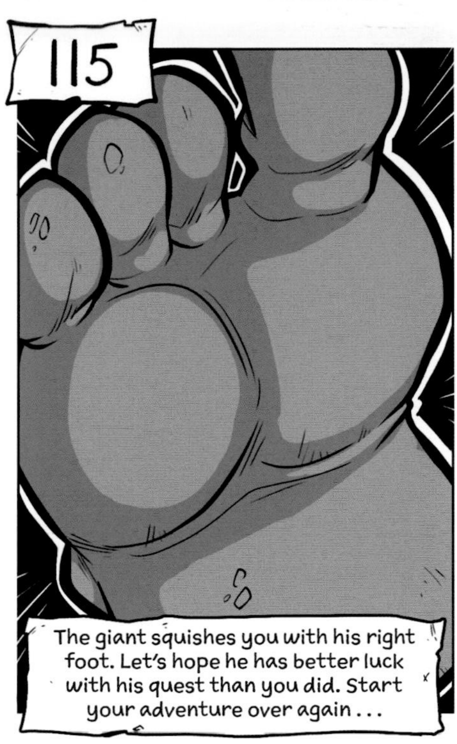
115
The giant squishes you with his right foot. Let's hope he has better luck with his quest than you did. Start your adventure over again . . .

116
96

117
47
218

118
=9
197

119

50 GP
10 GP
10 GP
10 GP
10 GP
5 GP
20 GP
50 GP
Knights Club
20 GP
10 GP
10 GP
10 GP
10 GP
20 GP
5 GP
50 GP
10 GP
50 GP
10 GP
EMPTY! 5 GP
20 GP
50 GP
5 GP
5 GP

When you've finished shopping, return to 69.

120

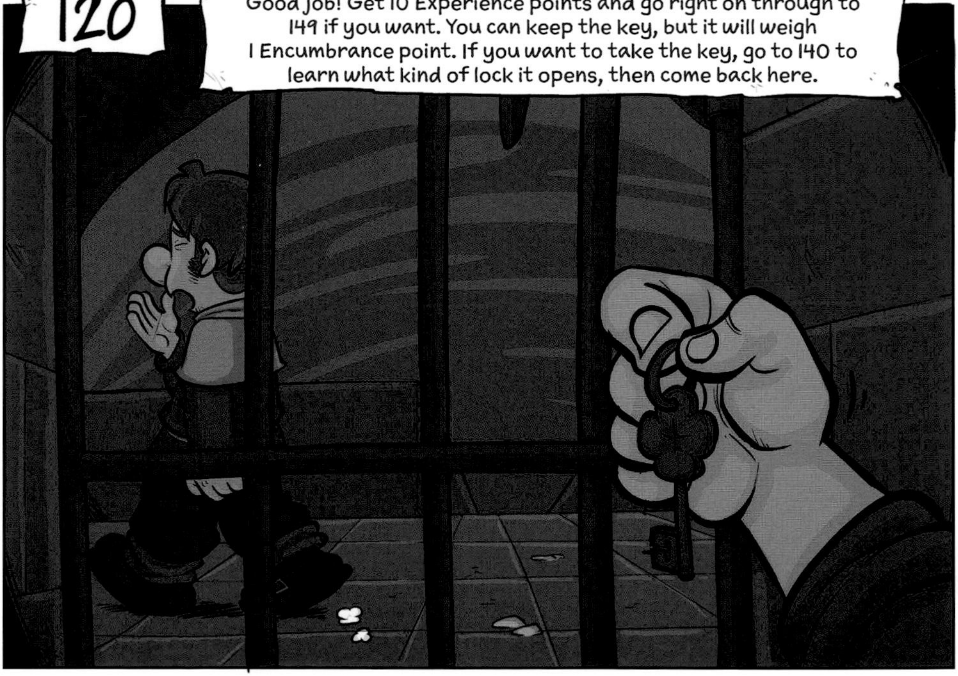

Good job! Get 10 Experience points and go right on through to 149 if you want. You can keep the key, but it will weigh 1 Encumbrance point. If you want to take the key, go to 140 to learn what kind of lock it opens, then come back here.

121

122

123

124

If you have at least 15 Strength points, you can pull the lever and proceed to 90. If not, open the door at 130. You can also retrace your way to 150.

125
185
34

126
This whistle lets you remove
1 search Star one time during
your adventure. Go back to 150.

127
63

128
141

129
17
133

130
177
105

131
17
95

132
166
So, if you got here without the lock-picking skill or the cat key, it has to be because you cheated. Return to 199 and lose 15 Experience points.

133

If you're here, you must be completely lost. I know you're looking for the city, and I can help you find it.

Give me something to eat or 20 gold pieces, and I'll take you . . . What do you say?

←95

129→

If you have some food or 20 gold pieces on you and you'd like the help, go to 113.

134

All right, all right. Respect. Now head back to 207.

135

You can go back to 209.

136

MULT	3		
SP	6	SQ	2
ATT	4		
RES	0		
SR	0		
XP	4		
LOOT	0		

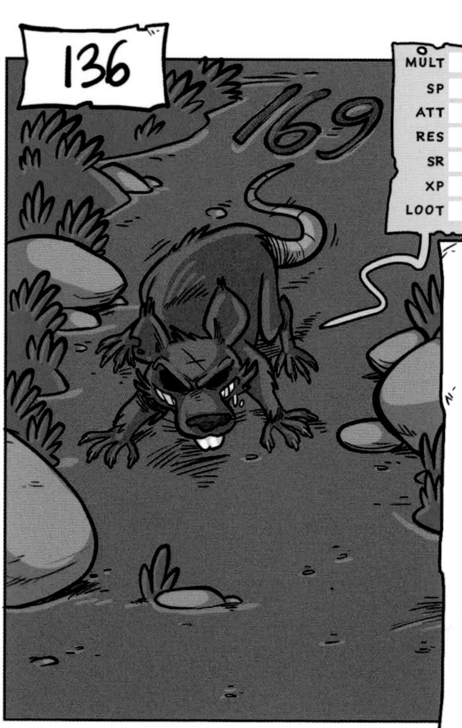

It's your first battle!

Use the wheel in the back of the book to fight, following the instructions on that page.

If you're a squire, only the XP box matters. Your Attack points must be equal to or higher than that number. If they aren't—run away!

You can choose to run away in any case (as you can for most battle encounters). You'll find out if fleeing came at a price in the next panel. If nothing is mentioned, you ran away without any trouble.

If you win, you win 4 Experience points, which you record on your Quest Tracker. If you're a squire, you win 5 gold pieces (GP).

Take note! If you're using your character from the previous adventure, you have to multiply everything by the multiplier (MULT), which in this case is 3. That gives this beast 18 Strike points and 12 Attack points, but doesn't give you extra Experience points or gold pieces, unfortunately.

137
31

138
You notice that two of the iron bars can be removed . . . It'd be too easy if I told you which ones. We'll meet up on the other side, or in 207 if you can't get it.

139
40

140
Warning! Only read the descriptions of keys you have or you'll spoil the game.
If you see a lock with a clover, you just have to add 131 to the number of the panel where you found it. Go back to your place in 120 or 62 after reading this.
If you see a door with a carving of the head of a serpent, subtract 86 from the number of the panel where you found it.

141

★

The guard hasn't seen you.

You can attack by spinning the wheel. If you get a hit, you win without having to fight. If you miss, the fight is on and your foe has time to raise the alarm. Your search counter goes up by 1 Star.

If you win, go to 81.

You could also choose to tap him on the shoulder and try to start a conversation by going to 29.

If none of these choices inspires you, turn back to 150.

MULT	4		
SP	11	SQ	3
ATT	8		
RES	1		
SR	0		
XP	8		
LOOT	10 Gold Pieces		

142

If you have greater than 15 Strength or Intelligence points, go to 46. If not, you have to solve this puzzle to enter. You can also turn back to 209, but you'll need to come back here again later. Otherwise, return to the entrance to the city in 150.

143

That worthless merchant is very much mistaken if he thinks I've forgotten his debt.

Anyway, I know perfectly well why you've come here, and why you're seeking my services.

Follow me to 27.

Marco's Place

144

You gain 20 Experience points. I hope that's enough for you to go up a level and add to one of your abilities. You're going to need agility to climb up these blocks! Go to 168.

145

If your search counter is exactly 5 Stars, a noise behind you gets your attention in 70. If you have less than 5 Stars, you advance peacefully to 221. If your counter is more than 5 Stars, that's because you cheated, right?

146

Looks like a dead end. Return to 150.

147

148

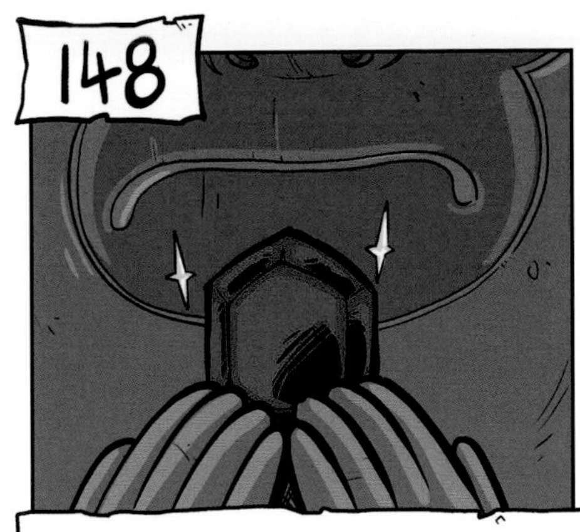

Unlike the other statues, this gem moves and might be able to come out. Nevertheless, after taking a good look (and mostly because I'm telling you!), you become certain that if you remove this stone without something to put in its place, a mechanism will activate. Needless to say, that doesn't bode well . . .

If you have an identical stone, whatever its color, you can switch them. Whatever you choose to do, go to 19.

149

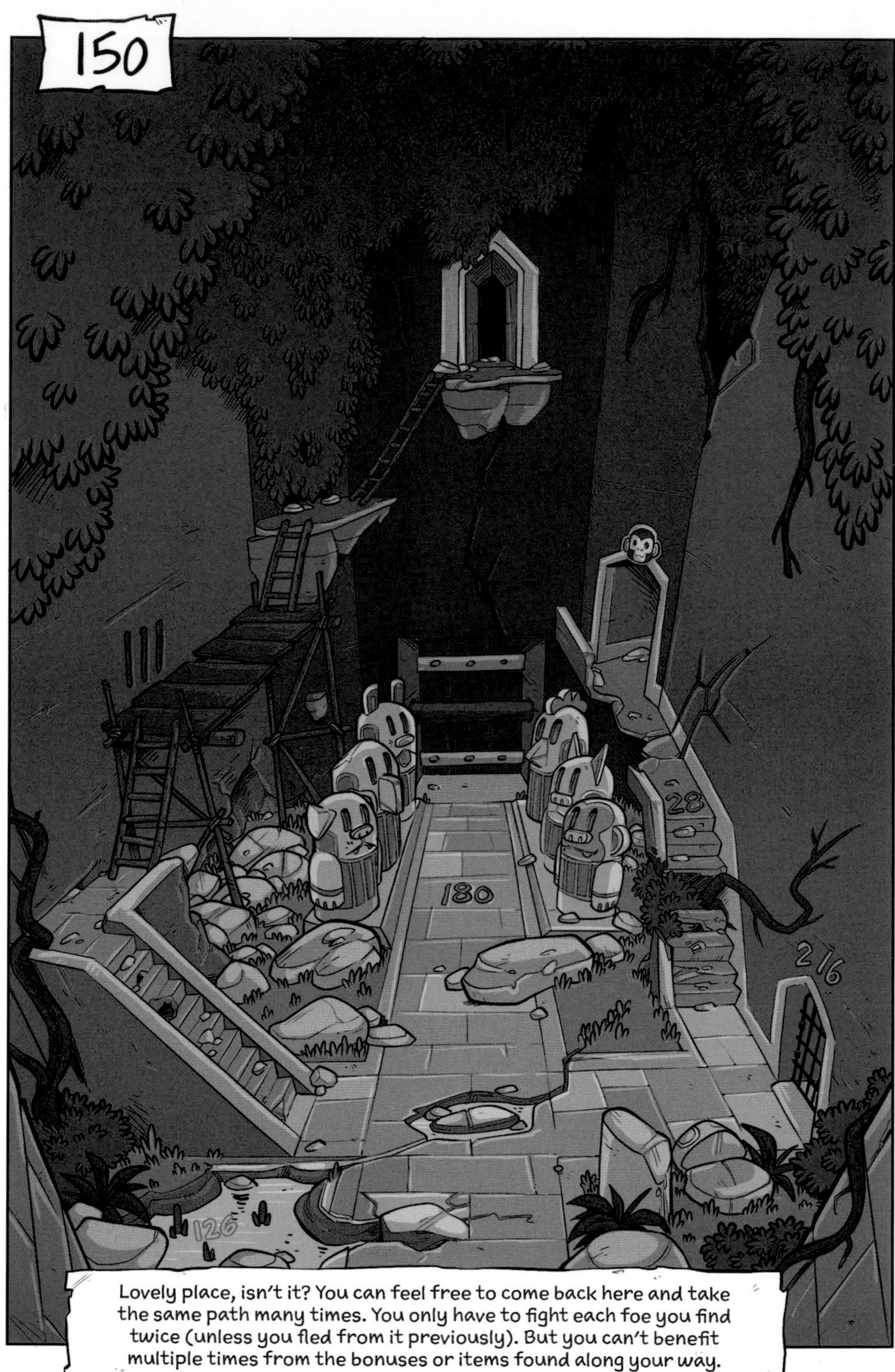
150
180
28
216
126
Lovely place, isn't it? You can feel free to come back here and take the same path many times. You only have to fight each foe you find twice (unless you fled from it previously). But you can't benefit multiple times from the bonuses or items found along your way.

151

80

106

152

Are you looking for potions? Hmm . . . Here's what I can offer you.

–Potion of 30 XP = 20 GP

–Potion of +2 Agility = 50 GP

–Potion of +2 Strength = 50 GP

–Potion of +2 Intelligence = 50 GP

If you have enough gold, you can purchase one or more potions. Their effect is permanent. Then go back to 150.

153

Thus ends the story of the gallant knight who defeated the most ferocious foes, who found dozens of bravery bracelets, and who accomplished a first mission with complete success. The weight of all the responsibility borne upon this knight's shoulders was too heavy, and so the decision was made, when least expected, to take to the sea on board this ship. The decision was irrevocable . . . It was time to retire and go lie in the sun . . .

(You can begin the adventure again.)

154

Nice view! Continue your climb in 183 or return to 150.

155

74

156

210

157

158

Good reflexes! Whatever your Strength, you slam the lid hard against the guard on the other side and stun him. You can defeat him (a second time) at your leisure and continue on your way in 102.

159

116

160
Here ends your adventure, knight. It's pretty clear that your visit has left its mark on the island and . . . Wait . . . Who is this man hailing you?
Paper, pen, fast! I must send a message as quickly as possible to an experienced adventurer!
Maybe we can help you?
?!
Ha ha ha!
I'm sure that if you search hard enough, you can find this island again!
Oh, uh, you were serious? Because I said "experienced" . . .
I also said "adventurer" so . . . uh . . . Thanks all the same.
WINK
The End
Shuky
WALTCH..
NOVY
03.14

161

You can turn back to 150.

162

163
To get out, you must jump on 3 blocks engraved with 3 exactly matching symbols. Put side by side, the numbers on those blocks will tell you where to go next. If none of the symbols rings a bell, all is lost. If you don't make it on the first try, it's barbecue for you (so again, all is lost). Good luck!

164

8

165

If you're an archer or a mage, you defeated the guard thanks to a well-aimed projectile without having to spin the wheel, so go to 36. If not, go to 103, but on tippy-toe.

166

If you got here by solving the puzzle, you get 20 Experience points.

209

167

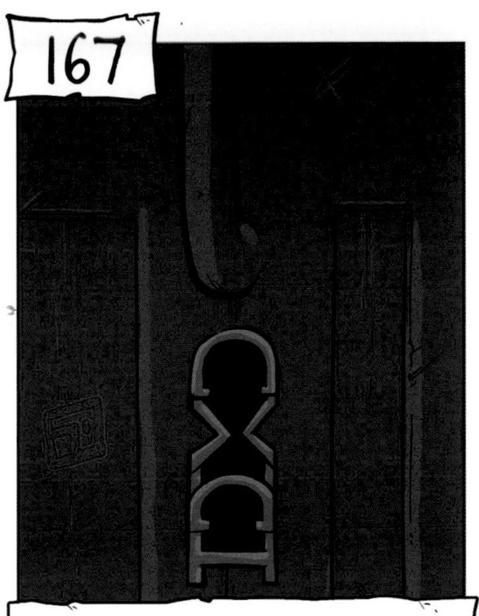

You can try forcing the lock—gently. If you have over 15 Intelligence or if you're a squire, go to 56. If you don't get it, go back to 150.

168

169

If you fled from battle, you lose 5 Strike points (5 gold pieces if you're a squire).

Note! If you started this adventure using your character from the last one, the multiplier (MULT) must be applied to the number of points or gold pieces you lose. So, you would lose 15 Strike points or 15 pieces of gold.

170

Take this letter to my girl. I've been at this post for many moons, and I miss her terribly. She works in the Hall of Alchemists. She's the only lady there, so you can't miss her. To deliver the letter, add up the values of the letters of her name when you get there.
Even though the instructions seem perfectly clear, here's a little help: A = 1, B = 2, etc. Now, go to 149.

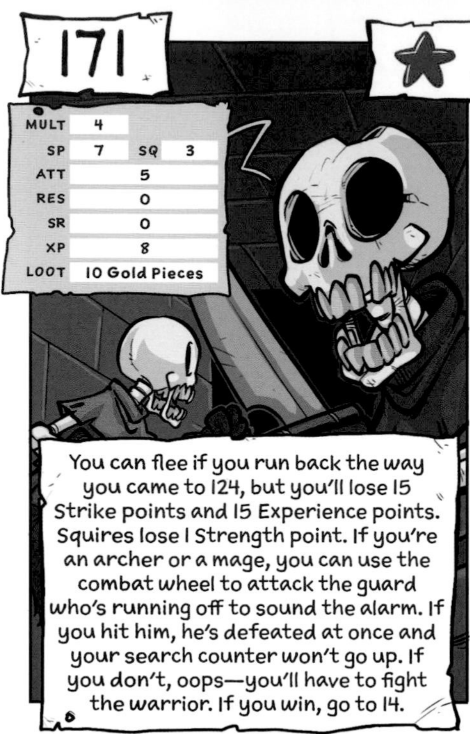
171
MULT 4
SP 7 SQ 3
ATT 5
RES 0
SR 0
XP 8
LOOT 10 Gold Pieces
You can flee if you run back the way you came to 124, but you'll lose 15 Strike points and 15 Experience points. Squires lose 1 Strength point. If you're an archer or a mage, you can use the combat wheel to attack the guard who's running off to sound the alarm. If you hit him, he's defeated at once and your search counter won't go up. If you don't, oops—you'll have to fight the warrior. If you win, go to 14.

172
58

173
51
I don't like the looks of this place. You could turn back and go to 104.

174

175
If you're coming from panel 25 and you've fled from a fight, you lose 5 Strike points (or 5 gold pieces if you're a squire). Note! If you started this adventure using your old character, the multiplier (MULT) is applied to the amount of points or gold pieces you lose.
106
55

176
8
Did you pick up some worker's overalls? Then you pass by unnoticed. If not, you raise the suspicions of this person, who goes at once to alert a guard to your presence. Your search counter goes up by 1 Star.

177
CLICK!
163
Uhh . . . What was that "click"???

178
I don't get it, so don't bother asking me. You can leave the temple and return to 104, unless you have another idea.

179

I don't think this is the hidden city Elliot told you about. Go back to 65.

180

181
Hurry up and jump in, knight! We can't stay here! Let's get to 219.

182
+20 SP

183
128

184
I don't think this guy needs that anymore. You find 20 gold pieces and a marvelous pair of boots that give you 1 extra Agility point. Return to 218.

185

MULT	3		
SP	7	SQ	2
ATT	4		
RES	0		
SR	0		
XP	4		
LOOT	0		

It's your first battle!

Remove the wheel from the back of the book, or spin a crayon or pencil around it. Follow the instructions on that page to fight.

If you're a squire, only the XP box matters. Your Attack points must be equal or higher than that number. If they aren't—run away!

You can choose to run away in any case (as you can for most battle encounters). You'll find out if fleeing came at a price in the next panel. If nothing is mentioned, you got away without any trouble.

If you win, you gain 4 Experience points, which you record on your Quest Tracker. If you're a squire, you win 5 gold pieces (GP).

Take note! If you're using your character from the previous adventure, you have to multiply everything by the multiplier (MULT), which in this case is 3. That gives this beast 21 Strike points and 12 Attack points, but doesn't give you extra Experience points or gold pieces, unfortunately.

186

187

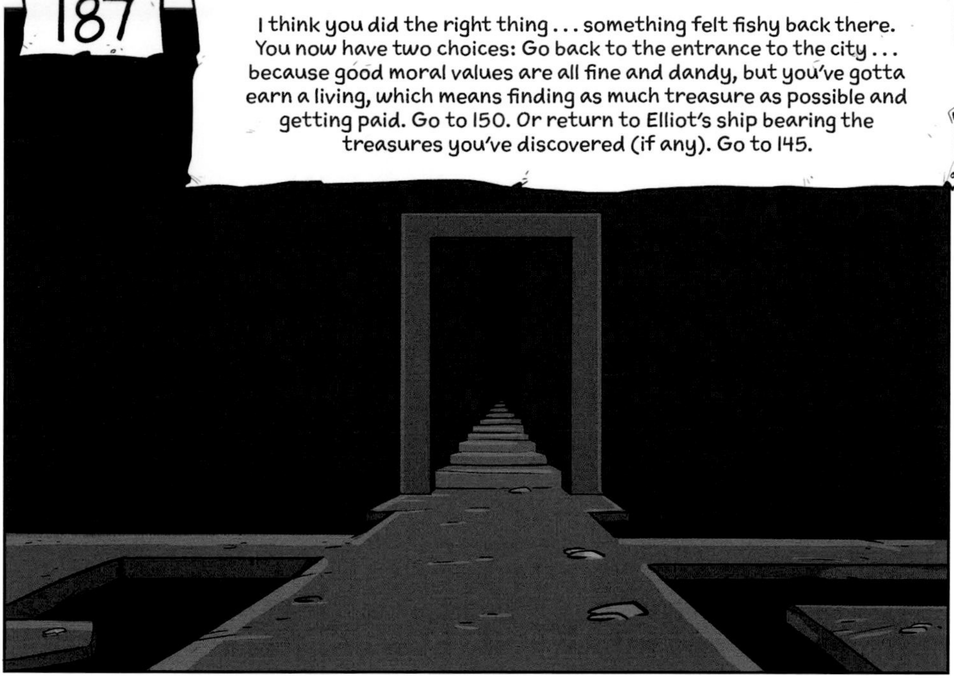

I think you did the right thing . . . something felt fishy back there. You now have two choices: Go back to the entrance to the city . . . because good moral values are all fine and dandy, but you've gotta earn a living, which means finding as much treasure as possible and getting paid. Go to 150. Or return to Elliot's ship bearing the treasures you've discovered (if any). Go to 145.

188

MULT	4		
SP	9	SQ	3
ATT	5		
RES	0		
SR	0		
XP	8		
LOOT	5 Gold Pieces		

You can decide to flee, but you will lose 10 Experience points and 10 Strike points. For squires, you lose 1 ability point. That makes you reconsider, doesn't it?

189

190

I can't help you here. What I can say is that you need to divide the number you get by 9 in order to open the door. If you can't solve it, go back to 15. (That'll be a nice hike. You'll lose 5 Strike points as well for how much road you'll have worn through.)

191

For opening this lock, you get 15 Experience points.

192

You can return to solid ground in 149 or let loose the mooring ropes in 153.

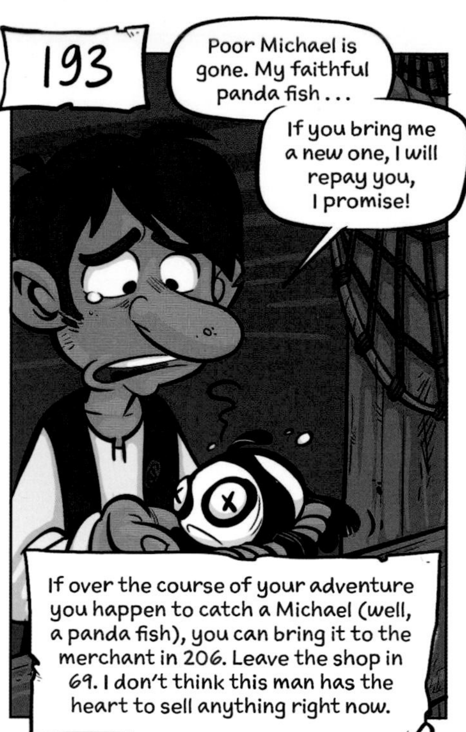

193
Poor Michael is gone. My faithful panda fish . . .
If you bring me a new one, I will repay you, I promise!
If over the course of your adventure you happen to catch a Michael (well, a panda fish), you can bring it to the merchant in 206. Leave the shop in 69. I don't think this man has the heart to sell anything right now.

194
Game over! A 500-pound door right on your head—that's gonna leave a mark! Start your adventure again . . .

195

The Legend of Wanosh

This is how the legend began, many millennia ago. This object, so beautiful and so terrifying, was in danger of being stolen from the Elk Clan. However, their chief, the bold Wanosh, tried everything to protect it from the bloodthirsty shadow knights, known for their hunger for power and conquest.

To their great surprise, the shadow knights were confronted by an army that, while few in number, was incredibly powerful. Indeed, in their magnificent armor crafted from precious metals, the Clan of Wanosh repelled the enemy, after fighting without rest for many moons.

In all of human memory, this was the first defeat of the shadow warriors, who were forced to flee whence they came, leaving many fallen behind on the island.

So says the legend that from that day on, Wanosh the All Powerful laid a curse on anyone who would dare fight against his people or attempt to steal the sacred stone. Through the use of his scepter, Wanosh trapped the bodies and spirits of his enemies, condemning them to watch over the city of the Elks for eternity.

Very interesting. You gain 1 point of Intelligence. Return to 150.

196
If that doesn't inspire you more, I can't do anything for you. Go to 218.

197

398

213

595

If you're respectful of the deceased and don't wish to disturb anything (or if you're just too squeamish), you can back out and go to 15.

198

Another foe . . . This one has an extra feature of 1 Resistance point. You have to subtract 1 point when you make a hit. If you have 5 Attack points, you will only cause 4 points of damage. Note! Adventurers using your character from the previous book: Don't forget to multiply by the multiplier (MULT). Your foe will have 3 Resistance points, 12 Strike points, and 12 Attack points. Start fighting!

MULT	3		
SP	4	SQ	2
ATT	4		
RES	1		
SR	0		
XP	4		
LOOT	0		

10

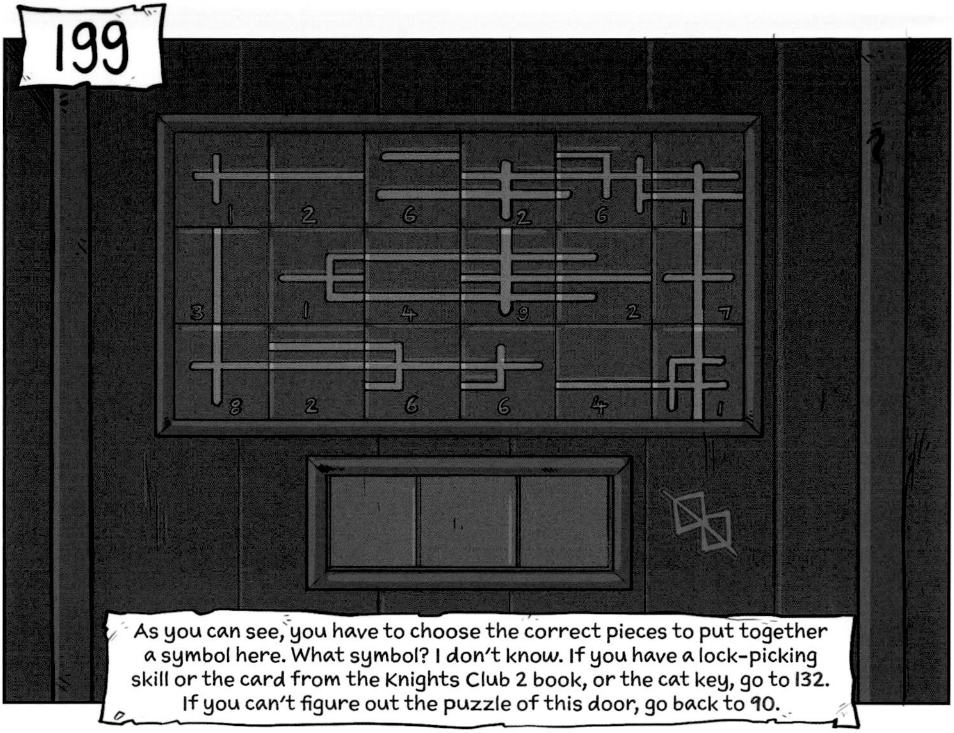

199

As you can see, you have to choose the correct pieces to put together a symbol here. What symbol? I don't know. If you have a lock-picking skill or the card from the Knights Club 2 book, or the cat key, go to 132. If you can't figure out the puzzle of this door, go back to 90.

200

You can choose to fight these two lumpy creatures in 115.
You can also attempt a calm and reasonable conversation in 61.

201
71

202
Thanks—I'll keep my mouth shut about you being here. Remove 1 search counter Star.
Hey . . . you wanna do me one more favor, buddy?
To say yes, go to 170. If you'd rather not, thank him for the help, then go to 149.

203
If you want to buy some potions, you'd better go see the Potions Master in 152.
Mirabelle

204
You bold adventurer! This for you!
This bracelet gives you 3 Strength points. Return to where you were before coming here.

205
107
You earn 30 Experience points for solving that riddle. Squires win 1 Attack point. Bravo!

206
Oh, what a magnificent specimen! Thank you, knight, thank you. I'll name this sweet little fishie Michael II.
As a reward, have this special fishhook.
Hold on! If you fished up Michael II in panel 23, you were mistaken . . . Turns out, it's not a panda fish, and the merchant notices this before you leave the store. He takes back the fishhook, and you lose 30 Experience points (30 gold pieces if you're a squire). Also, this fishing quest is canceled. Return now to where you were.

207
138
If you want, you can go back to 8.

208
I thought you looked like you could use some help! If you have 30 pieces of gold to give me, I'll show you which path to take. If that's what you want, go to 123.
9

209
142
87

210
The only way to get to Elliot's ship is
to find the number that will take you there.
Look carefully . . . but be quick!

211

Too bad! Part of the map is missing. But look—this will help you find the road leading to the hidden city. Now go back to 179.

212

213

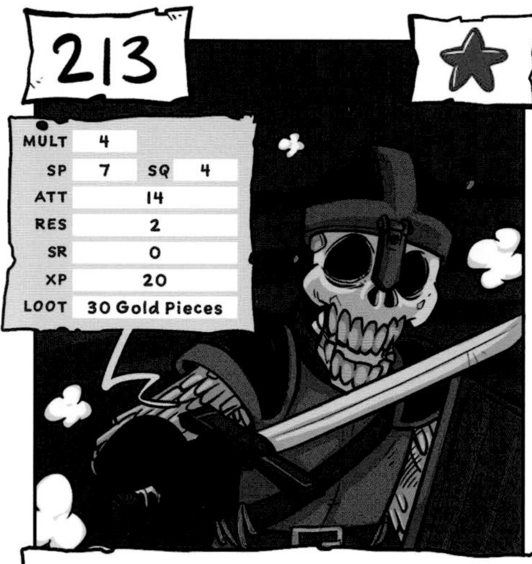

MULT	4		
SP	7	SQ	4
ATT	14		
RES	2		
SR	0		
XP	20		
LOOT	30 Gold Pieces		

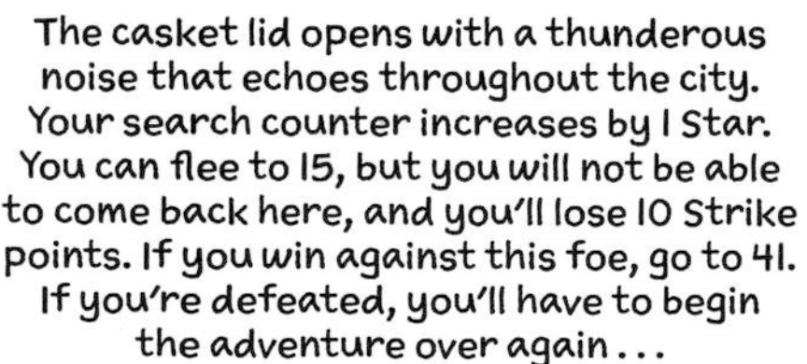

The casket lid opens with a thunderous noise that echoes throughout the city. Your search counter increases by 1 Star. You can flee to 15, but you will not be able to come back here, and you'll lose 10 Strike points. If you win against this foe, go to 41. If you're defeated, you'll have to begin the adventure over again . . .

214

If this is your first adventure in the Knights Club series, your bag contains 50 gold pieces. If you choose to buy this, flip to 223, then after that go to 69 to pick up some new gear.

Note: Do NOT look at the map in panel 224 before you've earned it!

215
If you have at least 13 Strength points, you can empty this cauldron and get this ring. If not, you can choose to stick your hand in the pot to get the bauble, but you'll lose 1 Agility point. Or you can be sensible and let it be. In any case, go back to 101.

216
If you can pick locks or if you have the wolf-head key, continue to 44. If not, go back to 150.

217
Concentrate and eliminate the extra numbers. Go back to 53 to solve the puzzle.

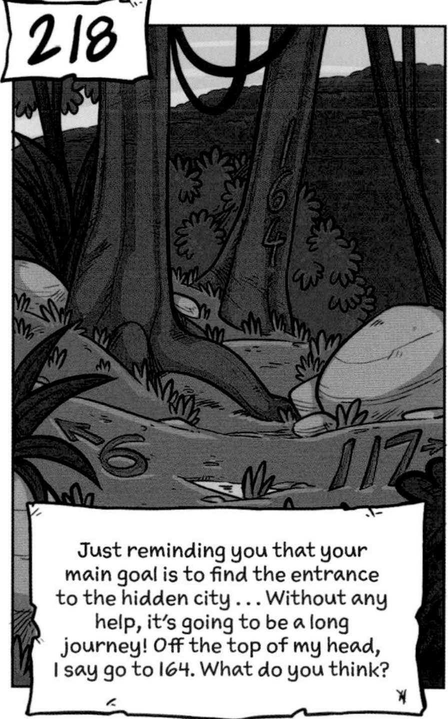
218
164
6
117
Just reminding you that your main goal is to find the entrance to the hidden city . . . Without any help, it's going to be a long journey! Off the top of my head, I say go to 164. What do you think?

219

Emerald-encrusted tiara:	25 points	Vase:	30 points
Eagle-headed scepter:	30 points	Glass bow:	50 points
Glass bow:	50 points	The Legend of Wanosh:	10 points
Black-iron sword:	15 points	The Elk Clan blade:	10 points
Pink-pearl necklace:	25 points	The Spirit ring:	10 points
Gold-thread bracelet:	10 points	The Tricky fishie hook:	25 points
Statuette:	5 points	The Golden platter:	15 points
Dog helmet:	35 points	The ring with three colorful stones:	10 points

If you have fewer than 50 points, go to A. If you have from 50 to 150 points, go to B. If you have 151 to 255 points, go to C. If you have more than 255 points, go to D.

Go to 160 if you brought back the ruby. If not, go to 220.

220
The End
Shuky
WALTCH..
Novy
03.14

221

222

Do you honestly think I have time to sign your books? I need to finish the next adventure! Leave me alone!

How to Write a Manuscript in 10 Easy Lessons

Perspective for Numbskulls

Primary Colors

223
N
W
E
S
RINCEPATÉDOUA

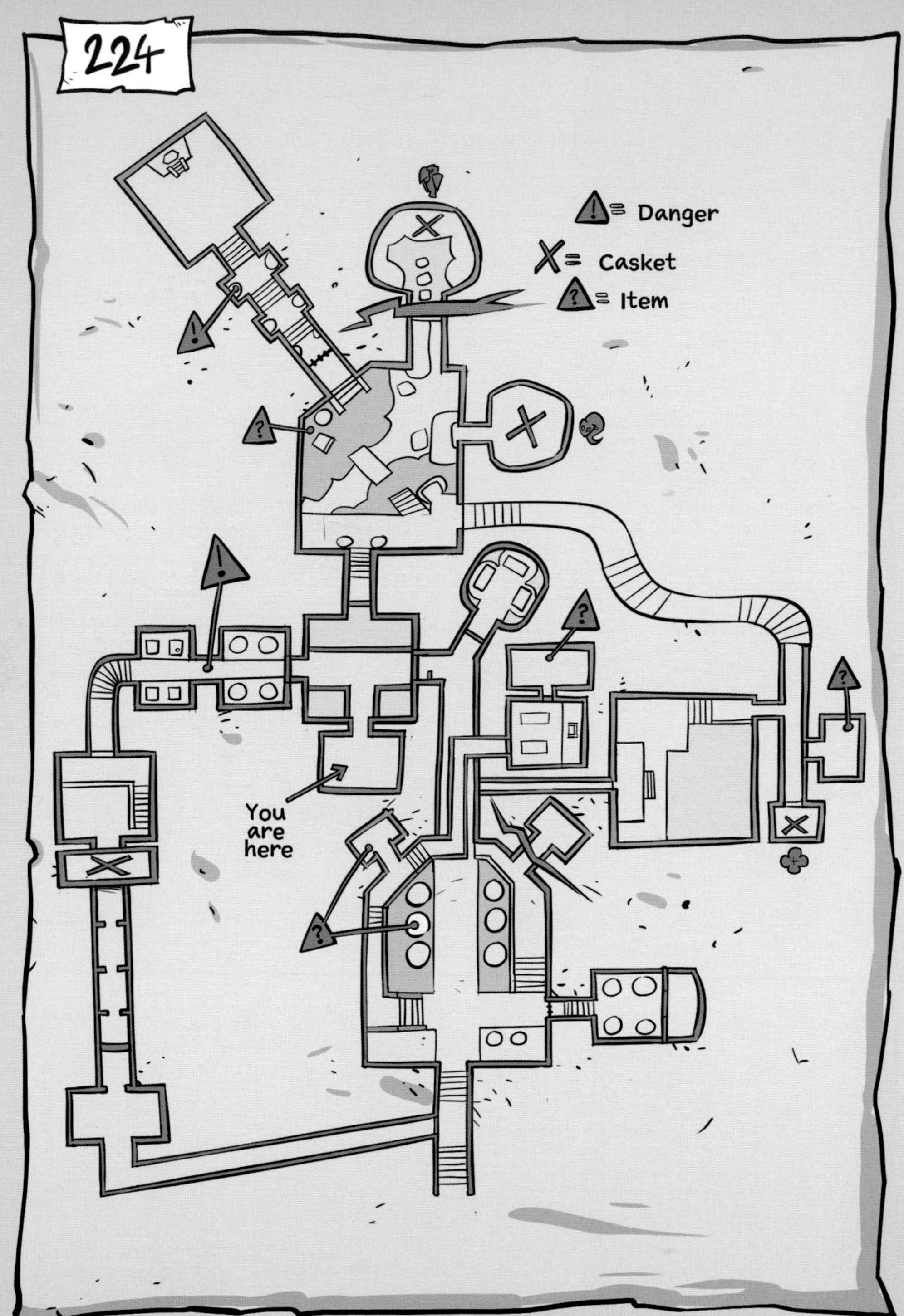

224
= Danger
= Casket
= Item
You are here

COMBAT WHEEL

Use this disk to fight the enemies you encounter on your adventure. If you are unable (or don't want) to cut it out, you can download one from comicquests.com. Then spin a pencil on top of the disk. Wherever the pencil tip stops is what you play.

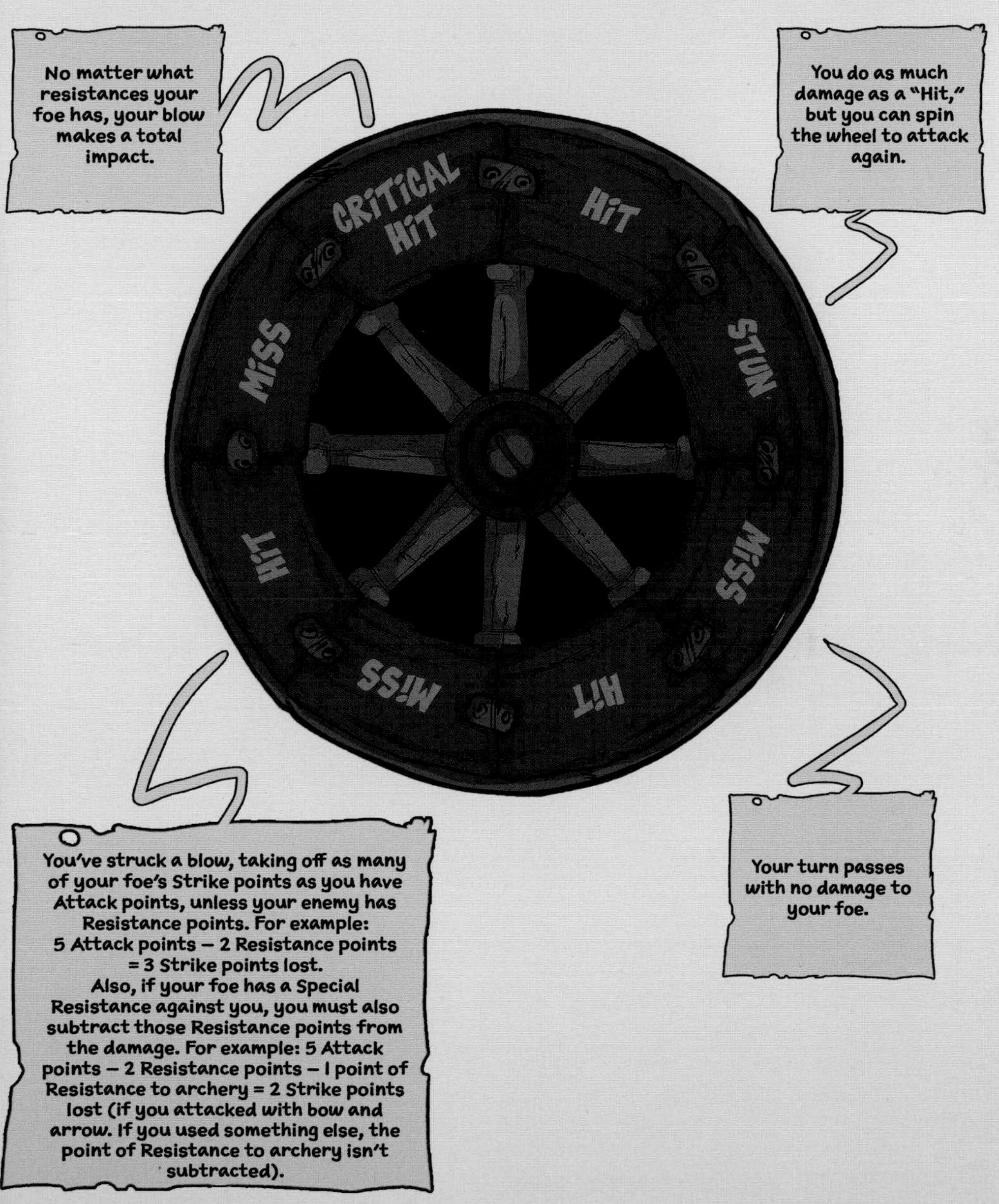

No matter what resistances your foe has, your blow makes a total impact.
You do as much damage as a "Hit," but you can spin the wheel to attack again.
CRITICAL HIT
HIT
STUN
MISS
HIT
MISS
HIT
MISS
You've struck a blow, taking off as many of your foe's Strike points as you have Attack points, unless your enemy has Resistance points. For example: 5 Attack points – 2 Resistance points = 3 Strike points lost. Also, if your foe has a Special Resistance against you, you must also subtract those Resistance points from the damage. For example: 5 Attack points – 2 Resistance points – 1 point of Resistance to archery = 2 Strike points lost (if you attacked with bow and arrow. If you used something else, the point of Resistance to archery isn't subtracted).
Your turn passes with no damage to your foe.

CRITICAL HIT
HIT
STUN
MISS
HIT
MISS
HIT
MISS